The Case of the Valiant Vizsla

A Thousand Islands Doggy Inn Mystery

B.R. Snow

This book is a work of fiction. Names, characters, places and events are either used fictitiously or are the product of the author's imagination. All rights reserved, including the right to reproduce this book, or portions thereof, in any form. No part of this text may be reproduced, transmitted, downloaded, decompiled, or stored in or introduced into any information storage and retrieval system, in any form by any means, whether electronic or mechanical without the express written consent of the author. The scanning, uploading, and distribution of this book via the Internet or any other means without the permission of the publisher are illegal and punishable by law.

Copyright © 2019 B.R. Snow
ISBN: 978-1-942691-60-0

Website: www.brsnow.net/
Twitter: @BernSnow
Facebook: facebook.com/bernsnow

Cover Design: Reggie Cullen
Cover Photo: James R. Miller

Other Books by B.R. Snow

The Thousand Islands Doggy Inn Mysteries

- The Case of the Abandoned Aussie
- The Case of the Brokenhearted Bulldog
- The Case of the Caged Cockers
- The Case of the Dapper Dandie Dinmont
- The Case of the Eccentric Elkhound
- The Case of the Faithful Frenchie
- The Case of the Graceful Goldens
- The Case of the Hurricane Hounds
- The Case of the Itinerant Ibizan
- The Case of the Jaded Jack Russell
- The Case of the Klutz King Charles
- The Case of the Lovable Labs
- The Case of the Mellow Maltese
- The Case of the Natty Newfie
- The Case of the Overdue Otterhound
- The Case of the Prescient Poodle
- The Case of the Quizzical Queens Beagle
- The Case of the Reliable Russian Spaniels
- The Case of the Salubrious Soft Coated Wheaten
- The Case of Italian Indigestion (A Josie and Chef Claire Sojourn)
- The Case of the Tenacious Tibetan
- The Case of the Unfettered Utonagan

The Whiskey Run Chronicles

- The Whiskey Run Chronicles – The Complete Volume 1
- The Whiskey Run Chronicles – The Complete Volume 2

The Damaged Posse

- American Midnight
- Larrikin Gene
- Sneaker World
- Summerman
- The Duplicates

Other Books

- Divorce Hotel
- Either Ore

To Dianne

For proving it's never too late for the dream

Chapter 1

I tucked Max under my arm and stifled a laugh as I watched the dogs watch Josie and Chef Claire spread a blanket out on the carpet then arrange four throw pillows in a circle on the outer edge. The dogs appeared to be supervising, and when they believed Josie and Chef Claire were done, glanced up at me with an expectant look. Max kicked her legs and held her arms out.

"I think everyone's ready," Josie said, laughing as she looked back and forth at Max and the dogs.

"We've created a monster," I said, shaking my head as I knelt down and gently placed Max on the blanket.

I sat down on the edge of the couch and watched the dogs take up their now normal positions. As if they were performing some sort of land-based, synchronized swimming move, the dogs stretched out and placed their heads on the pillows inches away from my daughter. Soon, Max was surrounded on all four sides by the dogs, and I couldn't miss the look of sheer joy on her face as she reached out with one hand and placed it on Captain's nose. The Newfie licked her tiny hand, and Max giggled with delight before managing to roll over and come face to face with Chloe, my Aussie Shepherd. Chloe nuzzled Max's hand as her tail ticked like a metronome.

Then Max did something that caught us by surprise. Using both arms for support, she pushed herself into a sitting position. When she realized what she had done, she giggled again and kicked her legs against the carpet.

"Wow," I said, staring at my four-month-old daughter. "I didn't see that coming."

"Me either," Chef Claire said, sitting down next to me. "Isn't it a bit early for her to be sitting up on her own?"

"They say it's anywhere between four and seven months," I said with a shrug.

"I told you she was an overachiever," Josie said.

Max wobbled then toppled forward and spent a few moments dealing with her facedown predicament. I immediately reacted and was about to insert myself when Max slowly pushed herself back into an upright position. Al and Dente, Chef Claire's Goldens, inched forward on the carpet and each licked one of Max's feet. That produced a round of giggles and she glanced around as if seeing the room for the first time.

"Strong kid," Chef Claire said.

"And smart," Josie said, then deadpanned. "I wonder who she gets that from."

"Funny," I said, making a face at her. "You know what this means?"

"That she'll be crawling before we know it?" Chef Claire said.

"Yeah," I said, studying my daughter's face as she looked around at all four dogs who were watching her closely and vying for attention. "They're so good with her."

"It's pretty amazing," Josie said. "But they've been that way since the day you brought her home."

We all stifled laughs as Max again started to fall forward but stopped herself by leaning backward. Then she toppled and landed on her back, blinked several times, then yawned, apparently worn out from the effort.

"She's already tuckered herself out," Chef Claire said.

"Well, we definitely know who she gets that from," Josie said with a grin.

"Don't you have work to do?" I said.

"Not until ten," Josie said.

"That reminds me," Chef Claire said. "We need to get another workout scheduled."

"Geez, Chef Claire," I said. "When I said I wanted to get in shape, I wasn't talking about Navy Seal shape."

"Just wait until we start working with weights," Chef Claire said, enjoying her comment way too much for my liking.

"You never said anything about weights."

"Oh, did I forget to mention that?"

"Unbelievable."

We heard a knock on the kitchen door followed by the sound of it opening. Moments later, my mother entered the living room and beamed at her granddaughter.

"There she is," my mother said, kneeling down next to Captain. She stroked the Newfie's head then leaned forward and picked Max up. "How's my girl today?"

"She just sat up on her own," I said, making room on the couch.

"Really? And I missed it?"

"I'm sure she'll do it again, Mom. You're early. I thought you were finishing up some stuff with the Arts Festival this morning."

"I'm done," she said. "It's called the power of delegation."

"Since when do you delegate?"

"Let's see," she said, stroking Max's head. "It's been about four months now." Then she cooed to her granddaughter. "Did you sit up all by yourself before

4

Grandma could get here?" Then she focused on me. "I have some exciting news for you, darling."

"Always a good way to start the day. Lay it on me, Mom."

"Dianne Harman has confirmed."

"Really?" I said, both surprised and delighted.

"Yes. She called this morning and said she was able to free up some time," my mother said.

"That's fantastic. I didn't think she was going to be able to make it," I said. "I mean, why would someone that famous take time out of her schedule to speak at a lowly arts festival?"

"I beg your pardon?" my mother said, raising an eyebrow at me. "Lowly?"

"No offense, Mom," I said, backpedaling. "But you must admit, it was a longshot getting her to come."

"Maybe," she said with a shrug. "But she's in Montreal at the moment. And I promised we'd take her fishing."

"She likes to fish?"

"Apparently," my mother said.

"It's been a while since she put a new book out," I said.

"Maybe she's dealing with writer's block," Chef Claire said.

"Or she's just tired," Josie said. "How many books does she have out?"

"It has to be close to fifty," I said.

"She writes them faster than I can read them," Josie said. "Or at least she used to."

"Well, whatever the reason is," my mother said. "Dianne said she decided to come when she realized I was your mother."

"What?" I said, confused.

"She wants to meet you. Apparently, she's heard about your crime-solving abilities."

"Where the heck did she hear that?"

"It turns out she's the aunt of a certain FBI agent," my mother said.

"Agent Tompkins?"

"That's the one," my mother said, gently rocking the now dozing Max in her arms. "We had a lovely chat. And I promised her you would take her fishing."

"Me?"

"Yes, darling. You. You haven't been out on the River all summer. It's time."

"Great idea, Mrs. C.," Chef Claire said. "She's developing a serious case of cabin fever."

"Geez, I don't know," I said, staring at Max.

"Max will be just fine with Grandma for the day," my mother said. "And spending some time on the River with one of your heroes is just what you need."

I gave the idea some thought, then nodded.

"A day on the River does sound good. When does she get in?"

"Tomorrow," my mother said. "You're meeting her and her publisher for lunch at the restaurant. But you'll need to eat on the verandah."

"Why's that?" Josie said.

"Because she's bringing her dog with her," my mother said.

"Cool," Josie said. "What kind of dog does she have?"

"A Vizsla," I said, then caught the looks they were giving me. "The dog is all over her website."

"They're gorgeous," Chef Claire said. "Hungarian hunting dog, right?"

"That's the one," Josie said. "They're really smart. And very trainable. As long as the owner is willing to put the work in."

"And they develop incredible bonds with their owners," I said.

"Even more than these guys?" Chef Claire said, nodding at the house dogs who were all sound asleep with their heads on the pillows.

"Yeah, as hard as that is to believe," Josie said, then frowned. "I think someone needs a change."

"Yes, I just noticed," my mother said.

"Here, I'll take care of her," Josie said, reaching for Max.

"Are you sure?" I said.

"Yeah, just sit there and relax," Josie said. "You can start working on all the questions you're going to torment the poor woman with."

"I don't torment…I inquire."

"Maybe she'll make you a character in one of her books," Claire said.

"That would be cool," I said, nodding.

"Geez, Max," Josie said, heading down the hall. "How does such a little thing like you manage to produce something like that?"

"She gets that from her mother."

"Funny, Mom."

Chapter 2

The restaurant, like the rest of Clay Bay, was
overflowing with people. Josie and I climbed the steps that
led to the wraparound verandah, and I paused on the top
step to take in the sights. Most of the downtown streets
were lined with popup canvas tents that served as
temporary homes for dozens of painters, woodworkers and
craft artisans. Other booths were occupied by a wide
variety of food vendors and the sights and smells produced
a smile that remained frozen in place.

"When your mom decides to put on an event she
doesn't miss much," Josie said as she glanced around.
"Great turnout."

"Yeah, she'll be happy with this," I said, taking a final
look around before turning my attention to the diners on the
verandah. "Are you sure she's going to be okay handling
Max by herself?"

"I like her chances," Josie said, gently punching me on
the shoulder. "She survived raising you, didn't she?"

"Funny."

"Remind me to pick up a sausage and pepper sandwich before we head home."

"Shouldn't you wait until after you've had lunch before you decide you want more to eat?"

"I'm skipping dessert," Josie said. "C'mon, let's find our table. I'm starving."

I followed her through the maze of tables, pausing several times to wave and chat briefly with friends I hadn't seen in a while and happily answered all questions about how the baby was doing. Then I spotted a woman casually sampling from a tray of appetizers and sipping wine as she chatted with her companions.

"That's her," I said, nudging Josie and nodding in the direction of the table. "I can't believe it."

"Let's try to keep the fan-girl stuff to a minimum, huh?"

I waved her comment away and made a beeline for the table. As I approached, the woman glanced up at me and smiled. She brushed a stray strand of hair away from her face and adjusted the silk blouse she was wearing. Her casual elegance and piercing stare immediately reminded me of my mother.

"Suzy?" she said, getting to her feet.

"That's me," I said, extending my hand. "It's so nice to meet you, Ms. Harman."

"Oh, please. We'll get along so much better if you call me Dianne."

"Dianne it is," I said. "This is Josie."

"The famous vet," Dianne said, nodding. "I've heard so much about your work."

We both frowned at the comment and glanced at each other.

"From your mother, primarily."

"Don't believe a word she says," I deadpanned. "She drinks."

"I'd love to stop by and see all your dogs," she said. "Your Doggy Inn sounds amazing."

"Sure, we'd love to give you a tour," I said, then spotted something draped across the writer's lap. "Speaking of dogs, who do we have here?"

I headed for the other side of the table and slowly extended my arm in the dog's direction. She was about sixty pounds and a gorgeous reddish brown from head to toe. After studying Dianne's reaction to our arrival, the dog sniffed my hand, glanced up at her owner then gently licked my hand. I responded by scratching the dog's head and ears. Josie followed suit and we took our time getting acquainted with the animal.

"She's gorgeous," I said. "Vizsla, right?"

"Very good," Dianne said, nodding. "You know your dogs."

"Well, she's all over your website," I said. "And we rescued one a couple of years ago." I turned to Josie who was still focused on the dog. "That sounds right, doesn't it?"

"Yeah," Josie said as she got to her feet. "Two summers ago. The dog bonded with Sammy. Stuck to him like glue."

"They do form strong bonds with their owners," Dianne said, then laughed as the dog inched even closer to her chair. "As you can see."

"What her name?" Josie said.

"Velcro."

We both laughed at the name, and I made a beeline for the chair next to the writer. Josie shook her head at me.

"Unbelievable," she said. "Behave yourself."

"I'm fine," I said, reaching for the bread and offering it to her. I took a piece and settled into my seat as I looked around. "Hi, everyone. Welcome to Clay Bay. I'm Suzy."

"Yes, I believe introductions are in order," Dianne said. "This is Suzy and Josie. They're two of the owners of the restaurant. And they run the Doggy Inn I was telling you about. I can't wait to see it."

"It's nice to meet you," Josie said, beaming at everyone before dredging her bread through olive oil.

"A pleasure," I said, nodding in agreement.

"Starting at the end of the table to my left is Joshua Jenkins," Dianne said. "He's a gifted mystery writer."

"Oh, I've read some of your stuff," I said, studying him. He was wearing jeans and a tee shirt and had a salt and pepper ponytail that ended halfway down his back. I found his books a bit predictable and syrupy, but this wasn't the time or place to mention it. "You're pretty good."

"Thank you," he said, nodding. "I'm here to promote my new book, so please stop by my booth at some point."

"Oh, I'll be there," I said, then focused on the woman sitting next to him.

"This is Selma Blankenship," Dianne continued. "My publisher."

"Mine too," Joshua said, raising his glass in salute.

Self-assured and alert, Selma casually raised her wine glass in my direction then took a long sip. I pegged her

13

image as corporate-cool which probably came in handy dealing with the demands of the publishing business as well as handling temperamental authors.

"It's nice to meet you," Selma said. "On my right is Imelda Enconi. She's my most trusted staffer. My go-to person whenever I need something done. Without her, not much would get done at Blankenship Publishing."

"Remember that the next time we're talking salary," Imelda said, sounding serious. Then she brightened and beamed back and forth at us. "It's nice to meet you. We took a boat tour this morning. It's a beautiful area. I had no idea this place existed."

"It's a special place," Josie said, then focused on the man sitting directly across from her. She extended her hand. "I'm Josie. It's nice to meet you."

"Same here," the man said as he returned the handshake. "Wilbur Smithers."

"Are you an author?" I said, shaking his hand.

"Heaven forbid," he said without emotion. "No, I'm a lawyer."

"Wilbur is Blankenship's lead counsel," Selma said, effortlessly sliding into the conversation. "He handles most of our author contracts and spends a lot of time on ancillary markets. You know, international rights, TV and film, stuff like that."

"Sure, sure," I said, nodding. "What brings you here?"

"Selma is punishing me," he said. "Says I need to get out of the office more. So, here I am."

"You poor baby," Selma said as she glanced around the table to emphasize her next point. "I thought it would be good for Wilbur to reconnect with some of our authors. It's easy to lose your perspective if you spend all your time on the 35th floor."

"Nice try, Selma," the lawyer said as he stirred the ice in his cocktail. "Moving on."

"Somebody touched a nerve," Josie whispered to me.

"Absolutely," I whispered back without making eye contact. I turned to Dianne and did my best not to gush. "I've been waiting forever for your next book. When is it coming out?"

"Hopefully, it won't be long," Dianne said, then snuck a furtive peek at Selma.

The publisher stifled a laugh before taking another long sip. Their brief, silent exchange caught my attention and I filed it away.

"I love your restaurant. Is it always this busy?" Joshua said.

"Pretty much," Josie said, reaching for another piece of bread. "At least during the summer."

"I've heard so much about your chef," Dianne said.

"From my mother, right?" I said, waving to our server as she approached.

"Yes, some," Dianne said. "But mostly from my nephew. He's quite taken with her." Then she chuckled to herself. "What a delicious name. Chef Claire."

"How is Agent Tompkins?" I said, reaching for another piece of bread.

"Apart from working far too hard, he's fine," she said, then sat back in her chair and smiled up at Bobbie, one of our servers.

"Hey, Suzy. Josie."

"Hi, Bobbie," I said. "What a zoo, huh?"

"Yeah, it's crazy. And a word of advice. I'd stay out of the kitchen for at least the next hour," Bobbie said with a laugh. "Chef Claire's in the zone."

Josie and I both nodded since we were very familiar with Chef Claire's intense focus when the restaurant was busy. People interrupting her Zen-like concentration while she was trying to fill dozens of orders did so at their own risk.

"I'd like to welcome all of you to C's," Bobbie said, passing out menus. She spotted the empty chair and looked at me. "Are you still for waiting for one more?"

"Geez, I'm not sure," I said.

"My agent," Dianne said.

"Mine too," Joshua interjected.

"But she's late as usual. Just leave the menu. She'll be here soon."

Bobbie took our drink orders then departed.

"I can't believe my mother convinced you to participate in a local arts festival."

"Actually, it wasn't that hard," Dianne said. "And I wanted to meet you."

"You did?"

"Yes. Your reputation precedes you," she said. "And I think you'd make a great lead character for a new series I'm planning. A fictionalized version of you, of course."

"Really?"

"Yes. Maybe we can talk about it later," the author said, then spotted a woman heading for the table. "There she is."

Everyone at the table focused on her as she made her way to the table. She came to a stop directly behind the remaining empty chair and stared down at it. She was rail-thin with jet black hair that belied her age, which I put somewhere around fifty. She frowned as she continued to study the chair.

"Oh, my," the woman said. "I'm not sure about this."

"For heaven's sake, Claudia," the lawyer said, shaking his head. "Please, just sit down."

"It's fine, Claudia," Dianne said, forcing a smile. "They're quite comfortable."

The woman slowly worked her way onto her chair and shifted back and forth several times until she was satisfied.

"Is she worried the chair is going to eat her?" Josie whispered.

"Don't start," I said, stifling a laugh. "Hi, Claudia. I'm Suzy. And this is Josie."

"It's nice to meet you," she said, giving us the briefest of looks before focusing on her menu. Then she looked up and addressed the table. "I'm sorry I'm late. One of the local artists has an amazing collection of kaleidoscopes in wooden telescopes. They're quite remarkable. It took me forever to decide which one to get."

"What did you end up getting?" Dianne said.

"Nothing," Claudia said. "I had too much on my mind to make a thoughtful decision. I'll stop by the booth later after my head clears."

18

The lawyer rolled his eyes and again swirled the ice in his drink before tossing back what was left.

"Good luck with that," he whispered to himself before picking up his menu. "What's good here?"

"Everything," Josie said.

"I think you'll like the food," I said.

"And if you don't, just let me know," Josie said. "I'll eat it."

I turned back to Dianne. "You really want to use me as one of your characters?"

"I do," she said, then finished her wine. "Maybe we can talk about it on our fishing trip."

"Perfect. If you're up for it, we'll head out after lunch."

"Oh, I would, but I'm afraid we have an afternoon meeting scheduled," Dianne said. "How about tomorrow morning?"

"Even better," I said. "You know, as far as catching fish goes. But we'll need to be out on the water by six-thirty at the latest."

"My, that's early," she said, frowning. "But I'm in. I'll just need to be back in time for my two o'clock presentation.

"That won't be a problem," I said, then turned to Josie. "You up for fishing tomorrow morning?"

"No can do," she said. "I'm booked solid all morning."

"Your loss," I said, then caught the look on her face. I followed her eyes and stared at the agent who was meticulously rearranging the place setting in front of her. Something about it was obviously distressing her and she appeared confused. "Is something wrong?"

"I'm lefthanded," Claudia said, holding her knife and fork in one hand and a water glass in the other. "I really should be sitting at the end of the table."

Wilbur, who was sitting in the seat in question, sighed loudly before getting to his feet.

"By all means, take my seat, Claudia," he said.

"Really?" she said.

"Anything I can do to help you find your focus," he said, taking a step back to give her room to slide into his chair.

"Thank you, Wilbur," Claudia said, beaming as she sat down. We watched her fidget non-stop until she eventually sat back in her chair and sighed contentedly. "Much better."

"Eccentric?" Josie whispered. "Or a total wingnut?"

"TBD," I whispered back. I glanced over at Dianne who was studying her agent with a sad smile. "How long has she been your agent?"

"Forever," the author said. "Unfortunately, that's the problem."

Chapter 3

I bounced Max on my knee as I watched Josie expertly chop vegetables for a salad. Max's attention seemed drawn to the rhythm of the knife hitting wood, and she gurgled contentedly as she jiggled both arms.

"You want a hand with anything?"

"No," Josie said, making a face at Max. "You just keep doing what you're doing there."

"She is a handful," I said, shaking my head as I lifted Max and held her close. "Aren't you?"

Max giggled and kicked her legs. I felt the familiar surge of unconditional love as I gently squeezed her.

"She's a happy kid," Josie said, then focused on the recipe in front of her. "What time did you tell everyone to be here?"

"Seven. I'll set the table after I get her down for a nap."

"Thanks. Just make sure I'm sitting far away from the weirdo," Josie said, looking up from her work to emphasize her point.

"Sorry, but she's all yours," I said, laughing. "She's left-handed, remember?"

"So?"

"My mom always sits on my right during family dinner," I said with a grin. "That only leaves the other end of the table. But you'll be fine. Just get her talking about kaleidoscopes. Or creative ways to arrange place settings."

"She must be good at her job," Josie said. "Because she would drive me nuts if I had to deal with her on a regular basis."

"She's quirky," I said.

"She a nutjob. Are you comfortable with the idea of being a character in a book?"

"Sure. Why wouldn't I be?"

"I don't know," Josie said with a shrug. "But I don't think I'd like it."

"That's because you're the most private person I've ever met."

"Nonsense. I'm just cautious," she said. "Who else is coming?"

"Well, my mom and Paulie will be here. And Rooster."

"Is Lacie coming?"

"No, she said she had something to take care of at the Lodge tonight. I think she's meeting with the guy who's building the fence around the hybrid sanctuary."

"Those two have become inseparable," she said, sliding the vegetables into a large wooden bowl. "You think they might decide to make it permanent?"

"Hard to tell," I said, nestling Max against my shoulder when she started to nod off. "But I think it's a possibility. They're an odd combination, but it seems to be working for them."

"It does," she said, checking her watch. "Okay, I'm going to get the ziti in. Remind me to put the chicken in the oven in half an hour."

"Will do," I said. "Or you could just set the timer."

"Nothing gets past you," she deadpanned.

"I'm going to get her down for a nap," I said, sliding off the stool.

"I'm going to open a bottle of wine," Josie said, wiping her hands on a dish towel as she scanned the wine rack next to the fridge.

I headed for my bedroom and gently placed Max in her crib. I watched her until I was satisfied she was sound asleep and headed back to the dining room. I set the table and jotted names on cards, chuckling to myself when I set

Claudia's card next to Josie's. Then we lounged in the living room and chatted about nothing as we sipped wine.

My mother and Paulie were the first to arrive, and we got them settled in with drinks while my mother peeked in on Max before eventually joining us.

"She's still out," my mother said. "But that makes sense. We had quite a play session this afternoon."

"Thanks for doing that, Mom. And you're still good to keep an eye on her in the morning?"

"I'll be here at six," she said.

"I'd be shocked if you weren't, Mrs. C.," Josie said.

We glanced up when we heard the soft knock on the kitchen door followed by Rooster's entrance.

"Good evening, all," he said, accepting the glass of wine Josie was holding out. "I brought a couple bottles of red. They're in the kitchen."

"Thanks, Rooster," I said. "I'm sorry Lacie couldn't make it."

"Me too," he said with a grin. "What are we having for dinner?"

"Ziti, breaded chicken cutlets and a salad," Josie said.

"Her loss," Rooster said.

"They'll be plenty," Josie said. "Take a plate for her with you." Then she gave him a coy smile. "Assuming you'll be seeing her later."

"Don't start," I said, laughing.

Then we heard a knock on the kitchen door.

"I'll get it," I said, getting to my feet.

I greeted the group we'd had lunch with earlier and escorted them into the living room. I handled introductions as Josie poured wine. After they got settled in, I couldn't miss their collective mood; a mixture of frustration and confusion tinged with anger. Josie noticed it as well and glanced over at me. I gave her a small shrug and pressed forward in an attempt to cut the tension filling the room.

"Did you get a chance to have some fun this afternoon?" I said.

"No," Dianne said, immediately taking the lead. "I'm afraid our meeting ran long."

"I hate when that happens," Josie said.

"You get used to it," Wilbur the lawyer said, then held his glass up to the light. "This is great wine."

"We had a bit of trouble sorting out a few issues," Dianne said softly.

Both Claudia and Selma snorted.

"Let's not do this again," Wilbur said as he examined the wine bottle. "Italian. I'm not familiar with this one."

"Stop the presses," Claudia said into her glass. "The lawyer admits to not knowing something."

Already desperate for a change of subjects, I turned to Dianne. "Where's Velcro?"

"Oh, I left him on my balcony at the hotel," she said. "He'll be fine."

"You should have brought him with you," I said. "He could have played with our guys."

"You keep dogs in the house?" Claudia said, glancing around nervously.

"They're downstairs in the game room," Josie said. "We'll let them out after dinner."

"How many dogs do you have?" Claudia said.

"Down at the Inn we have seventy at the moment," I said. "But we only have four house dogs."

"Only four," Claudia said with a frown. "That sounds like a lot."

"You'd think that," Josie said. "But not really. I have a Newfie. Suzy has an Aussie Shepherd, and Chef Claire has two Goldens."

"Great dogs," Paulie said, nodding. "All of them."

"And wonderful with Max," my mother said.

27

"Max?" Claudia said.

"My daughter. She's four months old. She's taking a nap but I'm sure she'll be up soon. Maybe we should eat while we have the chance."

"Great idea," Josie said, heading for the kitchen. "Rooster, you mind giving me a hand?"

"I live to serve," he said, following her.

"Let's head to the dining room," I said. "Just find your spot and have a seat."

Everyone, except Claudia, sat down at the table and settled in. Claudia remained standing with both hands clasping the back of her chair. She stared down at the chair, glanced off into the distance, then back down at the chair. She sighed loudly, uncertain about her next move.

"Problem?" Wilbur said.

"No," Claudia said then ran a hand through her hair.

"Please, Claudia," Dianne whispered. "Just take your seat."

Claudia nodded then slowly sunk into the chair next to Josie's and inched it closer to the table. I watched the scene play out from the other end of the table, again surprised by Claudia's demeanor as well as by the lack of reaction from the rest of her group. But I, along with my mother and Paulie, stared in disbelief at the woman.

28

"Does that chair have cooties?" my mother whispered as she leaned in close.

"I don't think so," I said, stifling a laugh.

Josie and Rooster arrived with dinner. They arranged the various dishes on the table then sat down.

"We usually do family style," Josie said, holding out a serving spoon to Claudia who eventually accepted it. "I hope you don't mind."

"Not at all," Dianne said. "It smells fantastic."

"Chef Claire's recipes," Josie said as she glanced at Claudia who had surrendered the spoon to Joshua sitting on her right. "Aren't you hungry?"

"I'm starving," Claudia said, gripping the sides of her chair with both hands. Then she ran both hands through her hair and vigorously shook her head. "No, I'm sorry. This just won't do."

We watched as Claudia got out of her chair and dragged it away from the table. She headed for the living room and returned lugging a leather footstool. She placed it where the chair had been, and I looked on in disbelief as she knelt on the footstool and wiggled forward on her knees until she was satisfied.

"Much better," she said to herself more than anyone else.

Josie, about to serve herself salad, put the tongs back in the bowl and a confused frown appeared, a look, I was sure, that matched my own. I continued to focus on Claudia, apparently content although she was now about a foot lower than everyone else at the table. She began spreading the napkin but stopped when she realized she didn't have any place to put it given her lack of a lap. Claudia tossed the napkin next to her plate and leaned forward with both elbows on the table. She watched the movement of the various dishes and maintained a reverent pose as she waited for them to make their way around the table.

"We usually just say grace," Josie deadpanned. "But whatever floats your boat."

"What?" Claudia said.

"Nothing."

"Holy crap," Paulie whispered. He speared a tomato wedge and did his best not to stare at the agent as he slowly chewed his food.

"I know," my mother whispered as she cast a furtive glance down the table at the agent who continued to closely monitor the movement of the dishes. "You don't think she's armed, do you, darling?"

"Now there's a cheery thought, Mom," I said, catching Josie's eye and giving her the slightest of shrugs. "I doubt she's packing, but just in case, I sure hope she likes the ziti."

"Should we make small talk?" my mother said under her breath.

"Knock yourself out, Mom. I got nothing."

"You invited them," she whispered through a small smile.

"Fine," I said, raising an eyebrow at her.

I cleared my throat and took a sip of wine. Deciding a safe topic was called for, I placed both elbows on the table and leaned forward.

"Dianne, I just have to know," I gushed. "When is your next book coming out? I can't wait. It's been so long."

Given the silence and death stares my question provoked, it was as if I had emptied a garbage bin in the center of the dining room table. I immediately sat back and felt my face flush.

"Yes, Dianne," Claudia said without looking up from organizing the food on her plate into individual bites. "When is your next book coming out? We're all dying to know."

"Claudia, please don't," Dianne said softly. She toyed with the food on her plate then glanced over at me. "It shouldn't be long."

Claudia snorted then took several moments to decide which bite was next. Eventually, she slid a forkful of ziti into her mouth. She chewed like a cow working on its cud and stared off at the wall with a smug smile plastered across her face.

"Actually, we were just talking about Dianne's next book at our meeting this afternoon," Selma said, seamlessly inserting herself into the conversation. "We've recently hit a few roadblocks. Hopefully, it won't be long."

"Yes," the lawyer said, nodding as he swirled the wine in his glass. "Roadblocks."

"Of other people's doing," Imelda said between sips of wine.

I had a ton of questions but decided they should wait. Unsure about how to ease the tension in the room, I was spared by Max who was making her presence known with a loud wail. I hopped up out of my chair and headed for the bedroom. Josie followed suit.

"I'll give you a hand with her," Josie said more to the table than me.

"Coward," I whispered with a laugh as she followed me down the hall.

"What was that all about?"

"I have no idea," I said, extending my arms as I leaned down to pick Max up. "Did you have a nice nap?"

Max bounced on the mattress and jiggled her arms. I lifted her and held her close to my chest.

"Somebody needs a change," I said, kissing her forehead then setting her down on the changing table next to the crib. I began my work and focused on Max who was staring up at the mobile above the table that was slowly rotating. "What's the deal with Claudia?"

"Like I said, she's a total nutjob," Josie said, gently running her hand over Max's neck and head. "Who organizes their food into individual bites?"

"Maybe she's on some sort of weird diet," I said, grimacing as I tossed the diaper into the receptacle next to the changing table. "You know, one that emphasizes portion control. Something like that."

"Or she's from another planet," Josie said, handing me a fresh diaper.

"A bit harsh, don't you think?"

"She's eating dinner while kneeling on a footstool."

"Yeah, there is that," I said, nodding as I fastened the diaper and picked Max up.

"You're getting good at that," Josie said.

"The key to excellence is practice and repetition," I said, laughing as I gently bounced Max in my arms. "Isn't it, Max?"

"Who said that?"

"Probably every mother on earth," I said. "Okay, Max, let's do your thing. If you don't give everybody something to talk about, I don't know what will."

Chapter 4

I was standing on the dock just before the sun peered over the horizon. But jagged streams of early morning light worked their way through the distant pines producing an irregular pattern of colors that blended into the serene surface of the water. The panorama reminded me of an enormous stained-glass window, and, as always, I was mesmerized by the view, a view I hadn't had much time to enjoy this summer.

I forced myself to focus and began loading the boat. It didn't take long and I resumed my distant stare. The stained-glass surface had already changed and was now taking on a distinct yellow tone as the sun finally emerged. When I heard the sound of tires on gravel, I turned and waved to Dianne as she climbed out of her rental and strolled toward the dock.

"Good morning," she called out with a wave.

"You made it," I said, remaining in the boat.

"I wouldn't miss this," she said. "I need a break from all the craziness."

I refrained from comment as I extended a hand and helped her climb into the boat. Then I untied the lines and fired up the engine. I backed out of the slip and pointed the boat toward deep water.

"There's a thermos of coffee in my bag," I said.

"Great," Dianne said. "You want a cup?"

"Yes, please," I said, scanning the water in front of me.

"This is so beautiful," she said, handing me a mug.

"It is," I said, glancing around with pride. "And it's going to be a beautiful day."

"What are we fishing for?"

"Bass," I said. "Smallmouth."

"Are they good?"

"I haven't eaten one since I was a kid," I said with a shrug. "But people seem to like them."

"You don't eat what you catch?"

"I hate the taste of fish," I said. "I only do catch and release."

"You spend hours trying to catch them, and when you do, you let them go?"

"Pretty much," I said, nodding.

"Interesting. I can use that."

"I'm sorry, but I'm not following."

36

"I'll make it one of your character's quirks," she said, glancing over with a grin. "You know, for my new series."

"You're serious about using me as one of your characters?"

"I am. I think you'll make a wonderful protagonist. If you're okay with it."

"Oh, I'm more than okay with it. I'm honored."

"Good. That makes me happy," she said, stretching her legs as she leaned back in her seat. She studied the passing shorelines comprised of various islands, both large and small, as if mentally cataloging the images. "I needed this. A welcome bit of serenity amid the turmoil of daily life."

"And no meetings, right?" I said, easing back on the throttle.

She flinched briefly but continued to smile.

"Is something on your mind, Suzy?"

"Well, it was a bit hard to miss the turmoil at dinner last night," I said as a simple statement of fact.

"Yes, I must apologize for all that. We weren't at our best."

"Can I ask you a question?"

"You're looking for permission to pry?" she said with a laugh. "Another quirk I can use. Go right ahead."

"What's the deal with Claudia?"

Her eyes narrowed and the smile disappeared.

"Claudia is…troubled," Dianne said softly.

I put the boat in neutral and turned the engine off. We began to drift in the current. I dropped anchor and checked the markings on the rope when it hit bottom.

"Forty feet," I said, securing the anchor rope to a cleat. "This is the spot."

"And you know this how?" Dianne said, peering over the side of the boat.

"There's a shelf about thirty feet below the surface," I said, pointing. "And the bass like to feed in the area, especially in the morning. At this time of year, the River gets a lot warmer and the fish head for deeper water. The current is strong down there, and it must be a great place for the bass to snack because they're usually here."

"I see," she said, accepting the fishing pole I was handing her.

"You know how to use that?" I said, grabbing my pole.

"I do. It's been a while, but I think I can manage."

I watched as she studied the reel and lure then looked back at me.

"Right over there?" she said, pointing.

"It's worth a shot," I said, casting. "Since we're using lures, I suggest you cast then slowly reel your line in. If we

38

were using live bait, we'd just cast and wait for a bite, but where's the fun in that, right?"

"You do this a lot?"

"As often as I can," I said. "But this is the first time I've been out all summer."

"Understandable," she said, slowly reeling her line in. "You're dealing with something much more important at the moment. Max is a beautiful little girl."

"Thank you," I said, reeling in the last of my line and immediately casting. "She's a handful but I have a lot of help."

"Your mother seems very involved in your life," Dianne said.

"That's a word for it," I said, laughing. "But she's great. A force of nature."

"Is she watching Max this morning?"

"Yeah, she loves spending time with her," I said, reaching for my phone. "That reminds me. I should give her a call. Crap."

"What's the matter?"

"I forgot my phone," I said, shaking my head.

"Would you like to use mine?"

"No, that's okay. My mom will just assume I'm checking up on her. It can wait."

I felt a tug on my line and gently pulled back in response to set the hook. Then I began to slowly reel my line in.

"You got one?" Dianne said, studying my movements.

"I do," I said, then spotted the bass when it broke the surface of the water. I reeled it into the boat and it flopped on the deck. "Oh, he's a nice one." I knelt down and carefully removed the hook from the fish's mouth and held it with both hands close to my face. "You should be more careful about what you eat. Back you go." I gently slid the bass back into the water.

"Do you always talk to the fish?"

"Yeah," I said with a shrug. "I should probably start working on that. You were saying that Claudia is troubled."

"Right to the point, huh?" Dianne said, expertly casting her line.

"Hey, you're good at this," I said.

"I used to fish with my dad when I was a kid. We had a place near Mammoth Lake in California."

"Nice," I said, nodding.

"It was," she said. "And such a long time ago." She drifted away on a memory then refocused. "Can I ask what happened to your husband?"

"He got hit by a bus on our honeymoon," I said, exhaling audibly as I choked back the emotion.

"Oh, my goodness," she said, sitting down. "I'm so sorry."

"Yeah…thanks. But please leave that out of my character's backstory. It would be…"

"Too hard to read about," she said, nodding. "A constant reminder."

"Exactly," I said, slowly reeling my line in.

"No problem."

"Thank you," I said, exhaling again as I scanned the horizon. Then I shook my head as if to clear the cobwebs and looked at her. "So, what makes Claudia troubled?"

"The rumors are true," Dianne said, laughing again. "You're like a dog with a bone." Then she focused on her pole. "I think I caught a fish."

"Just reel him in nice and slow."

"You sound like my father," she said, keeping her line tight as she reeled. Moments later, the bass was in the boat, and we both stared down as it flopped on the deck. "Now comes the hard part."

I watched as she picked the fish up with both hands and removed the hook. Then she slid it back into the water and wiped her hands on the towel I was holding out.

"Good job," I said. "No *trouble* at all."

"Okay, you win," she said, holding her hands up in mock surrender. "I'll talk."

"Let's take a break and have some more coffee while we chat."

We leaned our poles against the side of the boat and got comfortable on the padded seats that ran along both sides of the bow. I poured the coffee and handed her a mug. We studied our surroundings as we sipped, and the boat bobbed gently from a southerly breeze that was beginning to kick up.

"This place is magical," Dianne said. "How is it possible it's such a well-kept secret?"

"I think the winters have a lot to do with it," I said. "If it were like this year-round, the area would be overrun."

"That makes sense," she said. Then she took a sip before setting her mug down next to her. "Okay, Claudia. Do you have specific questions or should I just start talking?"

"Oh, I have a bunch," I said, laughing. "But you go ahead."

She stared off into the distance again then began.

"Claudia has always been a bit…quirky. At first, I found it charming, but over the years she's become exhausting."

"How long has she been your agent?"

"Years," Dianne said. "What's it been? Fifteen. No, it's coming up on sixteen."

"That's a long time," I said. "She's one of those people that gets your attention. And not necessarily in a good way."

"Yes, she has that effect on most people. I'm sure you saw it straight away."

"Well, her behavior at lunch was a bit strange," I said. "But when she knelt on the footstool during dinner last night, that pretty much sealed the deal."

"She recently added that one to her repertoire," Dianne said.

"What exactly is wrong with her?"

"I think the better question is what isn't wrong with her," Dianne said softly. "And I'm afraid she's getting worse. I seriously doubt if that's going to change in the near future."

I let the cryptic nature of her last statement pass without comment. But I filed it away to return to later if necessary.

43

"The way she organized the food on her plate was interesting," I said, gently probing.

"Now that is something she's been doing for quite a while," Dianne said. "She says it's the only way she can make sure there aren't any foreign objects in her food."

"Foreign objects?" I said, raising an eyebrow. "She's worried the Boogeyman might be hiding in her ziti?"

"Yes," she said, laughing. "Something like that."

"Does she have ADD?"

"She's been diagnosed with ADHD. Among other things."

"The H stands for hyperactivity, right?"

"It does," Dianne said. "At first, I assumed she was just a fidgeter. But it's much more serious than that."

"She seems to drift off at times," I said, remembering her behavior during dinner. "And then she'll snap at people. Bi-polar?"

"That appears to be the case," she said. "But I blame religion, as you put it, for the drifting off. Her constant exploration of different religions has clouded her thinking. You know, too many ideas that are all bouncing off one another."

"So, what is she?"

"This month she's into Hinduism."

"This month?" I said, raising an eyebrow.

"Her pattern is to dabble in different religions then move on when whatever faith she's following at the moment isn't delivering the results she expects. She went through all the major Christian faiths, settled in as a born-again for a while, then decided that Jesus just wasn't doing it for her. She moved on and went through stints with Buddhism, Islam, Shintoism, Scientology. You name it."

"She must be a well-versed religious scholar by this point," I said, tucking my legs underneath me on the seat.

"God, no," Dianne said, shaking her head. "Do you remember Cliff Notes from school?"

"Sure. If you can't be bothered reading the book, just buy the Cliff Notes version," I said, nodding.

"Well, when it comes to Claudia and the various religions she's been involved in, she's like the summary version of Cliff Notes."

"Eight miles wide and an inch deep?"

"Exactly," she said, then stared off toward the shoreline. "And when she burns out on Hinduism, I imagine her next stop will be atheism."

"So, she's a blamer?"

"Interesting," Dianne said, nodding. "Yes, I suppose you could say that. And as someone about to be the recipient of her blame, her wrath if you will, I need to be prepared for what she might do."

I studied her face closely and waited for her to continue.

"I've decided to make some changes," Dianne said. "And a big part of those changes will dramatically impact Claudia."

"You're going to fire her, aren't you?"

"I am," she said softly. "In fact, I already have. Just yesterday afternoon."

"Your meeting, right?"

"Actually, no. The meeting was about another matter. But I suppose it's all related. I told Claudia I was making the change after our meeting with Selma and her gang."

"I imagine Claudia didn't take the news well," I said.

"You saw her at dinner last night. What do you think?" Dianne said, her voice sharpening a notch.

"Got it."

"It's a mess," she said, then craned her neck out over the water. "It looks like we're about to have company."

"Yeah, this is a popular spot," I said, glancing over my shoulder. "But that's not a fisherman. That's Chief Abrams."

Chapter 5

I headed for the port side and gave the Chief a quick wave as I waited for him to arrive. He slowed down, then shut the engine off and coasted. I tied the boats together then extended a hand to help him on board.

"Playing hooky?" I said with a grin.

"I wish," he said far too seriously. "Sorry to interrupt your morning. How are they biting?"

"Good. I think," I said. "We each caught one then we started chatting."

The Chief nodded and focused on Dianne.

"You're Ms. Harman, right?"

"Yes. But please call me Dianne."

"Okay," the Chief said, nodding again. "I'm afraid I have some bad news."

"Crap," I whispered.

"What is it?" Dianne said.

"Selma Blankenship died in her sleep last night," the Chief said.

"What?" Dianne said, dumbfounded by the news.

47

"She was your publisher, right?" he said, removing a notebook from his pocket.

"She was. How is that even possible?"

"I beg your pardon?" the Chief said.

"Selma was a complete health nut," Dianne said. "Jogging, yoga, you name it, she did it. She was in amazing shape."

"Sometimes things just happen," the Chief said. "Had she been complaining about health issues lately? You know, headaches, chest pains, anything like that?"

Dianne gave the question some serious thought then shook her head.

"No. Nothing like that."

"When did they find her?" I said.

"This morning," the Chief said, checking his notes. "She was supposed to have breakfast with someone named Joshua Jenkins. And after she didn't show up, he called her room. When she didn't answer, he and a woman by the name of Imelda Enconi were escorted up to her room by the hotel manager. They found her in bed."

"I'm so sorry, Dianne," I said, as usual at a loss for words at times like these. "She seemed to be a nice woman."

48

"Yes," she said, staring off into the distance. "We go way back." She stared hard at the Chief. "Are you sure she died in her sleep?"

"As opposed to what?" the Chief said, raising an eyebrow at her.

She shook her head then folded her arms across her chest.

"I don't know," Dianne said. "It just seems odd."

"Our medical examiner is on site at the moment," the Chief said. "But it seems pretty obvious what happened. I know it's a shock, but like I said, sometimes things just happen."

"Of course," Dianne said, sitting down. "I'd like to see her if that's possible."

"I don't think that will be a problem," the Chief said. "I'll meet you at the Channel View. Again, I'm so sorry for your loss."

He climbed back into his boat and waited for me to untie the line. He accelerated and headed for Clay Bay. I followed his boat and focused on the water in front of me but kept glancing over at Dianne who was sitting quietly with her knees tucked under her chin, deep in thought.

"Are you okay?" I said, again coming up short and immediately feeling like an idiot.

"I just can't believe it," she said through teary eyes. "All that stress. And a lot of it was my fault."

"Stress?" I said, momentarily confused. Then I shrugged. "Sure, I get that. Running a major publishing company must be an enormous responsibility."

"It was. Especially these days. What have I done?"

I thought about her comment then the penny dropped.

"Does this have anything to do with your meeting yesterday afternoon?" I said, gently tossing the question out.

"I'm afraid it might have everything to do with it," she said, wiping her eyes with a tissue.

Despite my neurons firing on all cylinders, I forced myself to remain silent. She needed time to deal with her loss, and all my questions could wait. But it wasn't easy. I focused on the morning sun and the impact it was having on the shoreline as I sped past. Ten minutes later, I pulled into a slip at the dock in front of the Channel View, a high-end hotel popular with both tourists and locals. Aptly named because of the magnificent view it offered of the River, we climbed out of the boat and took a few moments to take in the sights as we waited for the Chief to finish scribbling in his notepad.

50

"Okay," he said. "Just remember not to touch anything in her room."

We left the dock and headed for the main entrance where a small group of somber hotel staff were standing near the elevator chatting quietly. I gave them a small wave and forced a smile as we walked past them. As we waited for the elevator, the staff dispersed and headed down a long hallway that led to the dining room.

"I think the news is out," I said, nodding at the departing staff.

"Yeah, word travels fast," the Chief said, pushing the up button again.

"You know that doesn't make it come any faster, right?" I said.

"I know," he said, staring at the elevator door. "But it gives me something to do."

"Ah, the illusion of control," I deadpanned.

"Don't start."

"Sorry."

Mercifully, the elevator finally arrived, and we shuffled inside and leaned against separate corners. We rode in silence to the seventh floor and the Chief held the door as Dianne and I stepped out. We walked the length of the hall until we reached the door of the Admiral Suite. The

Chief knocked softly and moments later Freddie, our local medical examiner, opened the door and waved us in.

"Hey, Suzy," he said, then focused on Dianne. "It's so nice to meet you, Ms. Harman. I just wish it could be under better circumstances. I'm a big fan."

"Thank you," Dianne whispered as her eyes scanned the suite. "Is she in the bedroom?"

"She is," Freddie said. "Much to George's displeasure, I haven't moved her yet."

"George?" Dianne said.

"The hotel manager," Freddie said. "He's anxious for us to finish up. For obvious reasons."

"Are you waiting for the paramedics to collect the body?" the Chief said.

"No, they're here," Freddie said. "But I needed to wait until you got back. I sent them downstairs to have some breakfast."

"You needed to wait?" the Chief said with a frown. "I don't like the sound of that."

"Oh, you caught that," Freddie deadpanned then motioned for us to follow him into the bedroom. "C'mon. I've got something to show you."

"Crap," I whispered.

"What?" Dianne said.

52

"Nothing."

We entered the bedroom and spotted Selma Blankenship's body stretched out on the bed, her body covered by a sheet except for her head. A stunned, wide-eyed expression was frozen in place and I had to force myself to look at her. But Dianne was only able to sneak brief glances at the woman. Then she began to shake and weep. I helped her into a chair next to the bed and handed her a box of tissues.

The Chief and Freddie were both closely studying the dead woman without touching her, and as soon as Dianne was settled in, I joined them bedside.

"What do you see?" Freddie said to the Chief.

"Her neck is swollen," he said, leaning down close to woman's head. "And I see some red splotches on both sides."

"Splotches?" Freddie said. "You getting technical with me, Chief?"

"You're worse than her," the Chief said, nodding in my direction as he stood upright.

I leaned in closer for a better look and couldn't miss the swelling and the marks that reminded me of tiny varicose veins. If varicose veins were red.

"Her blood vessels burst?" I said.

"That's my best guess at the moment," Freddie said.

"Is that normal?" I said.

"It's common enough," Freddie said. "When breathing stops, there can be an enormous buildup of pressure. And, eventually, all that blood needs to go somewhere."

"But the swelling around the neck isn't normal," the Chief said.

"Not if her death was from natural causes," Freddie said softly. He let his comment hang in the air and glanced back and forth at us. "I'm betting whoever killed her used that pillow her head is resting on."

"Her killer?" Dianne said, hopping up out of her chair. "Selma was murdered?"

"It's a distinct possibility," Freddie said without emotion. "I can't explain the swelling any other way. And she must have put up quite a fight given the amount of trauma to her neck. I have a feeling she didn't go down without a struggle."

"No, I'm sure she didn't," Dianne said, staring down at the body. Then she caught the look we were giving her. "I mean, if you knew Selma, you'd understand what I mean by that. She was very tough when necessary. And she hated not being in control of every situation."

"Any idea who might want to kill her?" the Chief said.

"All her competitors and probably half her writers," Dianne said with a shrug. Then she again responded to our stares. "I'm speaking metaphorically, of course. She was well known as a ruthless businesswoman."

"But it must have been someone she knew, right?" Freddie said. "You know, for the killer to be in the room."

"I doubt if she let someone in she didn't know," the Chief said, then spotted me heading for the sliding glass doors that led to the balcony overlooking the River. "Where are you going?"

"Just checking something," I said, coming to a stop directly in front of the doors. "Let's take a look. Did you bring gloves with you?"

"What am I, an amateur?" the Chief said, shaking his head as he pulled on a pair of latex gloves.

"I was just asking," I said, making a face at him. "There's no need to get snarky."

"I always get snarky when my plans get ruined," he said, examining the curtains with one hand. "I was hoping to spend the day at the arts festival."

He pulled the curtains apart and sunlight filled the room.

"The safety dowel is in place," he said, kneeling down for a closer look.

I glanced down at the object, a round piece of wood about three feet long inserted into the track at the bottom of the door.

"Yeah," I said, nodding as my neurons flared. "Let's take a look at the door from the outside."

The Chief removed the dowel then slid the doors open. A burst of cool air enveloped us, and I stepped outside onto the balcony. The breeze whipped my hair and I put my hands on my hips as I looked around. Then I focused on the outside latch.

"Do those look like scratches to you?" I said.

"They do," he said, studying the door. "Penknife. Maybe a screwdriver. But they could have been here forever."

I nodded then walked to the end of the balcony and leaned forward. Then I dug through my bag for my phone. A thick book was blocking my hand and I removed it and tossed it on a nearby table before continuing my search.

"Is that the new Connelly?" the Chief said.

"Yeah, it's fantastic." Then I stopped searching when I remembered I didn't have my phone. "Dang it."

"Problem?"

"I don't have my phone."

"Don't worry, we'll get lots of photos," the Chief said.

"It's only about four feet from the balcony next door," I said. "What do you think?"

"About whether somebody could have come over from there?" he said, taking a good look at both balconies.

"Yeah."

"Sure. You'd have to be a bit of an athlete, but it's certainly possible."

"Or someone in a total rage determined to make it happen."

"You got somebody in mind?" the Chief said, studying my expression closely.

"Maybe."

"But even if you're right, if somebody did climb over the balcony, how did they get past the safety dowel?"

"Good question, Chief."

"Thanks. That's why they pay me the big bucks."

"Maybe somebody removed the dowel earlier."

"Possible," the Chief said, nodding. "And after they took Selma out, they put it back, locked the sliders and went out through the front door. I can make that work."

"Me too," I said. "That supports the theory somebody was in the suite with her at some point during the day. Or last night."

"It does," he said. "How many people are here with her?"

"Let's see," I said, doing the math. "Well, obviously Dianne. Dianne's agent, Claudia, Selma's assistant, her Chief Counsel, and Joshua Jenkins. The guy she was supposed to have breakfast with."

"I've read a couple of his books. He's okay. But a little sugary for my taste."

"They all had a meeting yesterday afternoon," I said, rubbing my forehead. "I don't think it went well."

"Interesting. What was it about?"

"I don't know. Yet."

The Chief snorted and shook his head as he stared out at the view.

"Amazing view from up here," he said. "Selma must have been doing pretty well. This suite isn't cheap."

"No, it's not," I said. "Okay, what now?"

The Chief gave it some thought then motioned for me to follow him back inside. Dianne glanced up at us with an expectant look.

"What did you find?" she said.

"Not much," the Chief said. "We were just exploring the possibility the killer came in from the outside."

"And?" Dianne said.

"It's a possibility. But it's too soon to tell," he said. "Freddie, would you mind giving Detective Williams a call and ask him to stop by?"

"You got it, Chief. Where are you going?"

"I need to head downstairs and have a chat with George," he said. "He's not going to be happy with what I'm about to tell him." He focused on Dianne. "I'll need to speak with you and the rest of your travel party later on."

"Of course," Dianne said, then flinched. "Oh, my goodness. I completely forgot. I need to take Velcro out so she can take care of business. That's okay, isn't it?

"Velcro?"

"My dog."

"Cool name," the Chief said. "Just stop back when you're done. We'll be here."

"Thank you, Chief Abrams," Dianne said, then glanced at me. "You feel like taking a walk?"

"You took the words right out of my mouth."

59

Chapter 6

We left the suite and headed down the hall to Dianne's room. We were greeted by a very excited Velcro who said hello to me then focused exclusively on her owner. Then the dog calmed down momentarily, apparently remembering she needed to pee, and headed for the door.

"Hang on, Velcro," Dianne said with a laugh as she headed for the bathroom. "I just need to wash my hands."

While I waited, I headed outside to her balcony and scanned the layout that ran the length of the western side of the hotel. Each room had its own balcony and a three-foot, wrought iron barrier separated them. Deciding that anyone with a reasonable amount of athletic ability could easily scale each barrier and make their way to the channel-facing end of the hotel where Selma's suite was located, I filed the information away and walked inside where Dianne was waiting with the bouncing Vizsla.

"We better get her out," I said, laughing as I nodded at Velcro. "She's busting."

"She is," Dianne said, reaching down to stroke the dog's head. "You ready to go?"

"Lead the way."

We walked to the elevator and the doors opened immediately. Two paramedics appeared and they both forced a smile at us.

"Hey, Suzy."

"Hi, Jimmy, Shorty," I said, making room for them to get off the elevator.

"End of the hall, right?" Shorty said.

"Yeah. The Admiral Suite," I said.

They gave us a small wave and headed down the hall. We rode the elevator down to the lobby and walked outside where bright sunlight greeted us. Dianne glanced at me as if waiting for directions.

"Let's head down that path," I said, pointing. "It leads to a nature trail that runs along the River."

Dianne nodded and knelt down to remove Velcro's lead. The dog immediately trotted to a nearby patch of lawn and took care of business. Then the Vizsla returned and nuzzled Dianne's legs. She leaned down to pet the dog then began walking.

"She's a great dog," I said. "Has she always stuck that close to you?"

"Ever since she was a puppy," Dianne said. "We have an incredible bond. It's hard to explain. A lot of people don't understand it."

"I get it," I said, glancing around as we strolled the tree-lined trail. "Chloe, my Aussie Shepherd, is the same way." Then my neurons surged as if urging me to get on with it. I rubbed my forehead and took a quick look at the morning boat traffic before focusing on the author. "Can I ask you a question?"

"Sure," she said, keeping a close eye on Velcro who was exploring her surroundings. "Given what I'm sure is coming later, it'll be good practice for me."

"Chief Abrams and Detective Williams are both very thorough," I said, nodding. "But fair."

"Detective Williams?"

"He's with the state police." I fell silent for several moments as we strolled the path before continuing. "What was your meeting about yesterday?"

"It was about the end of the beginning," she said, coming to a stop. "A mid-career reset, so to speak."

"I think I'm going to need a bit more," I said, motioning at a park bench we were about to pass.

We both sat down and the Vizsla spotted our movements and immediately raced over, hopped up on the bench and rested her head in Dianne's lap. I couldn't help but laugh and I reached out and scratched the dog's ears.

"I've decided to make some serious changes," she said, rubbing the dog's head.

"Like firing Claudia?"

"Yes, among others. Actually, removing Claudia as my agent is almost secondary to my major change."

"You're terminating your relationship with Selma's company, right?"

"You're good," she said, glancing over at me.

"Thanks. I have my moments," I said, processing the latest information. "And yesterday's meeting was focused on your leaving?"

"It was. One of many meetings we've had over the past several months," she said softly.

"I imagine it's complicated. You've been with Blankenship for a long time."

"Eleven years," she said. "And they've been very good to me. At least they have been in the past."

"My guess is there are some sticking points about your departure?"

"To say the least," she said, acquiescing to the dog's request for a tummy rub.

"It has to be contract related, right? You know, what's holding things up?"

"It is," she said, nodding. "I have one book remaining on my current contract. A book I submitted to Blankenship eight months ago."

"That's the reason you haven't released a book in over a year?"

"That's it," Dianne said, brushing hair away from her face as the breeze kicked up.

"I thought you might be dealing with writer's block," I said.

"No, actually I've been writing like crazy the past year. Including the book I submitted to fulfill the last of my contractual requirements, I have five ready to go."

"Five?" I said, relishing the prospect I might soon have several new books to enjoy. "You have been busy."

"Yes. I have the first four books in a new series ready to go," she said, her mood brightening for the first time all morning. "I'm very happy with it."

"What's the argument with Blankenship about?" I said. "It seems pretty straightforward. You gave them the last book you owed them."

"That's what I thought. But there's some language in my contract that, according to the lawyers, is a bit vague."

"That can't be good," I said, frowning. "I've found that unclear contracts are the lifeblood of many lawyers."

"Lifeblood," she said with a chuckle. "I like that. I've been using the analogy of two dogs fighting over a bone."

"So, what's the problem?" I said, draping my arm over the back of the bench.

"Blankenship doesn't want the book I submitted," Dianne said. "Actually, to be more specific, they want another book more."

"The first book in your new series, right?"

"Yes. They know it's going to be a successful series, and they believe, once I see how well it does under their imprint, I'll change my mind about leaving."

"What's the book you submitted to them about?"

"It's the final installment in my Cove Archives series," she said.

"Oh, I love that series," I said. "I was wondering if you were going to do another one."

"There were some loose ends to tie up before I finally said goodbye to those characters," Dianne said, then noticed the Vizsla's intense focus on a nearby squirrel. "No, Velcro. Just leave him be. He's not bothering anybody."

65

The dog cocked her head and stared up at Dianne before dropping it back onto her lap. I laughed at the familiar sight.

"Blankenship didn't think the Cove series warranted another book?" I said.

"They'd be happy to publish it," she said. "But only if I agree to their demand that they have right of first refusal on book one of the new series."

"How could the contract be that unclear?" I said.

"That's a very long story."

"All the good ones are," I said with a shrug.

"Indeed," she said, laughing. "It's my second contract with Blankenship. And the first one went off without a hitch. I thought the second would go as smoothly. And it did until I decided I wanted out."

"Can I ask why you decided to leave?"

"Money. And more control over my books," she said, exhaling audibly.

"Your new publisher is giving you that?" I said, confused.

"Oh, I'm not signing with another publisher," she said. "My plan is to set up my own company and go independent."

"Interesting," I said, nodding. "I've heard a lot of authors are doing that."

"They are," Dianne said. "And I've talked with a lot of them. Technology has made the traditional publishing model rather obsolete."

"I have a friend, a famous musician, who explained what technology has done to the music business," I said. "I imagine it's doing the same thing to the publishing industry."

"It is," Dianne said. "It's created major and, in all likelihood, permanent disintermediation."

"Hey, if you're going to start using words like that, I'm so out of here," I said, laughing loudly.

"Sorry. Disintermediation is the reduction and often removal in the use of intermediaries between producers and consumers."

"You're talking about removing the middleman."

"That's it," she said. "As an independent, I can publish directly to Amazon and my readers can buy my books with one click."

"The Mighty Zon," I said, nodding. "No need to hop in the car and head to a bookstore, right?"

"If you can even find a bookstore," she said. "I explained it to Selma several times, and I know she understands…understood what I was talking about. But I'm one of her most popular authors and Blankenship is already in enough trouble. The fact is I simply don't need a publisher these days."

"Or an agent?" I said, raising an eyebrow at her.

"Exactly," she said, nodding. "Especially one who doesn't pay attention to contractual terms."

"Claudia missed the right of first refusal clause?"

"We both did," she said. "She assured me there were no issues with the contract. But in the end, it's still my fault for not catching it."

"How heated did yesterday's meeting get?" I said, steering the conversation back in the direction it needed to go.

"You mean, did anyone get angry enough to kill Selma?"

"Yeah. That's the question."

"There were a lot of harsh words. From several people in the room," Dianne said. "But murder? All our relationships have taken a major hit, but that's quite a stretch."

"Selma must have made you some sort of counter-proposal," I said.

"She did. But she couldn't come close on the royalty percentage or the degree of control I'm looking for," she said, glancing down at the Vizsla who was sound asleep and snoring softly.

"Who do you think killed her?" I said, after checking my watch and deciding it was time to address the elephant in the room.

"I'm afraid my detective skills are confined to fiction," she said with a shrug. "I have no idea."

"Well, whoever did it had obviously given it some thought," I said.

"Why do you say that?" Dianne said, studying my face closely.

"I think the killer came in through the balcony," I said. "That indicates premeditation. And using a pillow to smother Selma was an obvious attempt to make it look accidental. And if her neck hadn't swollen the way it did and burst the blood vessels, that's probably how the police would have classified it."

"Interesting," she said.

"It would have been a bit of a challenge to get onto the balcony," I said. "But it's very doable. And as soon as the killer knew what room Selma was in, it wouldn't have taken long to put a plan together."

Dianne flinched and the dog immediately hopped to its feet. Velcro stared intensely at her obvious distress and gently pawed her leg. I stared at the look of shock on her face in disbelief. I tried to wait it out, but her expression remained fixed in place.

"Geez, Dianne. What the hell is the matter?"

"Selma's room," she whispered.

"What about it?"

"It was previously mine."

"What?"

"I was given that suite when I checked in," Dianne said. "But Velcro wouldn't stop barking at all the boats going by. I got a call from the manager telling me that some of the guests were starting to complain. So, I asked Selma to switch rooms with me."

"Geez," I whispered as my neurons surged. "Who knew you guys switched rooms?"

"I didn't say anything. But I suppose Selma could have mentioned it," she said, then gave me a wide-eyed stare. "That means I could have been the intended victim, doesn't it?"

"Let's not jump to any conclusions," I said, already jumping to several of my own. "We need to talk to the cops."

I got to my feet and checked my watch again.

"After that, I need to get home and check in to see how my mom and Max are doing."

"Of course," Dianne said, slowly getting to her feet, her face still ashen.

"And I need to have a chat with my mom about how to go about canceling your presentation this afternoon."

"No," she said, shaking her head. "I want to go ahead with it. Your mother said she's expecting several hundred people."

"I'm not sure that's a good idea, Dianne. As soon as word gets out about Selma's death, if somebody was trying to take you out, they might try again."

"In front of several hundred people?" she said, again shaking her head. "I'll take my chances."

I couldn't miss the serious tone in her voice, so I filed my protests away.

"Okay, it's your call," I said eventually.

"It's better than saying it's my funeral, right?"

"Oh, let's not even go there."

Chapter 7

We took the elevator to the top floor and Dianne put Velcro back in her room before we headed down the hall to the suite. The Chief and Detective Williams were chatting quietly and both glanced up when we entered.

"Hey, Detective Williams," I said, extending my hand.

As always, when dealing with situations such as these, he was solemn and composed.

"Hi, Suzy," Detective Williams said, then focused on Dianne. "Ms. Harman?"

"Yes, but please call me Dianne."

"Will do. I'm Detective Williams with the state police. I'm so sorry for your loss. We have some questions we'd like to ask, if that's okay with you."

"Certainly," she said. "Do you mind if I sit down?"

"Good idea," the Chief said. "Let's all sit."

We settled into a couch and chairs in the living room of the suite, and I craned my neck into the bedroom where Freddie and the two paramedics were preparing the body for departure. Then I remembered what was about to happen and glanced back and forth at the Chief and the detective.

"Should I leave?" I said.

"No, you're fine," Detective Williams said, opening his notebook. "Based on what we've seen so far, we're probably going to need all the help we can get."

"What have you found?" I said.

"Just this," the Chief said, holding up a small plastic bag with an object inside. He handed it to Dianne who studied it closely. "Does that pen look familiar?"

"Actually, it does," she said, handing it to me. "But I can't remember where I've seen it."

The pen was black with an ornate gold pattern on the cap. I handed it back to the Chief who slid the bag into his pocket.

"Looks expensive," I said.

"Yeah," the Chief said. "It was under the bed."

"You think it fell out of the killer's pocket?" Dianne said.

"It's certainly possible," Detective Williams said, then gave Dianne his best cop stare. "Do you have any idea who might have wanted to kill your publisher?"

"Apart from me, not really," Dianne blurted with a shrug.

73

"Are you trying to be funny, Ms. Harman?" Detective Williams said. "Because if you are, this really isn't the time or place."

"I'm sorry," Dianne said, her face flushed with embarrassment. "It's just that Selma was making my life a living hell."

"Let's start with that," Detective Williams said, sitting back and draping a leg over his knee.

Dianne took several minutes to tell the same story she'd told me outside. But the version she told the cops included a lot more detail. I listened closely as she outlined the events of the past several months and fought the urge to jump in. A list of questions quickly developed in my head, but I patiently waited until she finished her story.

"And your meeting yesterday didn't go well?" the Chief said.

"No. It was more of the same. Just more intense than the others," Dianne said, then flinched when the paramedics left the bedroom carrying a black body bag. "Oh, my." Then the floodgates opened and she began sobbing.

We sat quietly waiting as she dabbed at her eyes. Eventually, she exhaled and nodded she was ready to continue.

"Can you think of anything else you need to tell us at the moment?" Detective Williams said.

Dianne glanced over at me and I nodded. She nodded back and focused on the two cops.

"Selma and I switched rooms yesterday," she said softly. "I was originally staying in this suite."

Detective Williams and the Chief stared at each other before focusing on Dianne.

"Why did you do that?" Chief Abrams said.

"My dog was barking at all the boats going past," she said. "And the guests were starting to complain."

"I see," Detective Williams said, scribbling in his notebook. "Who in your party knew you had changed rooms?"

"I have no idea," she said. "Do you think it's possible someone was trying to kill me?"

"Not until two minutes ago," the Chief said.

"Geez, this changes things," Detective Williams said, glancing at the Chief. "What do you think?"

"I think we should keep talking," the Chief said.

"How much longer will we be?" Dianne said. "I need to do some final prep for my presentation this afternoon."

"You're not going to cancel?" the Chief said, surprised by the news.

"No, I'm not. I have several hundred people coming to hear me," she said. "It wouldn't be fair to them."

Both cops gave it some thought then shrugged it off. I glanced at my watch and got to my feet.

"I need to run."

"Okay," the Chief said. "Are you coming to Dianne's presentation?"

"I wouldn't miss it," I said, forcing a smile at her. "I'll see you later. Hang in there."

"Thanks, Suzy," Dianne said.

"I'll walk down with you," the Chief said, following me to the door.

"I imagine I'll see you later, too," I said to Detective Williams on my way past him.

"I'd be shocked if I didn't," he said without looking up from his notebook.

"Funny."

The Chief and I strolled down the hallway in silence and waited for the elevator. As we rode down, he looked over at me. My neurons were on fire and it took me a few moments to notice his piercing stare.

"Penny for your thoughts," he said with a laugh.

"Cheapskate."

"I'm a lowly paid public servant," he said with a shrug. "What have you got?"

"Not much," I said. "I'm just wondering how much harder it's going to be to find a killer when we're not even sure who the intended victim was."

"Based on my experience, a lot," he said. "Do you think she's capable of murder?"

"Dianne? No way," I said, shaking my head. Then I caught the look on the Chief's face. "Do you?"

"She does spend all her time figuring out clever ways to kill people," he said.

"And then she writes it down. That's a long way from actually killing somebody, Chief."

"It is," he said. "But I'm keeping her on the list for now."

"Do you really think a woman her age could have made that climb from one balcony to the other?"

"No, I don't," he said softly.

"There you go," I said, doing my best not to sound annoyed. I stepped into the lobby when the elevator doors opened and waited for him to continue the conversation.

"Your assumption that someone came over the balcony," he said.

"What about it?"

77

"If you're wrong, it could change everything," he said.

"The victim was asleep, Chief. It's not like she heard a knock on the door, let whoever it was in, then went back to bed."

"No, you're probably right," he said softly. "That's not plausible at all."

I stared at his poker face and scowled.

"Why do I get the feeling you're slow walking me to an epiphany?"

"Good word. But you forgot one distinct possibility."

"Only one?" I said. "That's not bad."

He laughed and it broke the tension.

"Well?" I said eventually.

"What if Dianne never returned her keycard to the suite?" he said.

"Crap," I whispered. My mind ran wild for several moments before I got it under control. Then a question floated to the surface and I smiled at the Chief. "But she's pretty old to be smothering someone with a pillow, right?"

"She is," he said, nodding. "But we've seen the effects of intense rage all too often. What do you call it?"

"The adrenaline coma," I said. "No way, Chief. I'm not buying it."

"I'm not necessarily buying it either. All I'm saying is that it's a possibility. She said herself how difficult Blankenship was making her life."

I was officially on overload and felt the onset of a headache. I rubbed my forehead and exhaled audibly.

"I need to get home," I said, reaching for my car keys. "I'll see you at the auditorium."

"Try not to overthink it," he said.

"I don't like my chances. You will have extra security there just in case, right?"

"We will," he said, then turned fatherly. "Look, I know she's one of your heroes, but try to keep an open mind, okay?"

"As soon as I make some room, I'll do my best, Chief."

I gave him a long hug then headed for my car. I made the short drive home, hopped out and did my best lumber to the kitchen door. Obviously having heard my car arrive, all four house dogs greeted me as soon as I entered. I spent some time saying hello to them then noticed Chloe's expectant stare at the door. I let all four out to take care of business then headed for the living room. I came to a sudden stop when I spotted something that made my heart melt. My mother was sprawled out on the couch on her back with Max tucked against her chest. Both were sound asleep but before I could take a picture, my mother opened her eyes and blinked several times.

"Hello, darling," she whispered as she glanced down at the baby. "I must have dozed off."

"How long has she been asleep?" I said, sitting down on the adjacent couch.

"About an hour," my mother said, doing her best not to disturb Max's rest.

"Any problems?" I said, staring intensely at my daughter.

"She was an angel," my mother said, stifling a yawn.

"She gets that from me," I deadpanned. "Where's Paulie?"

"He and Rooster went fishing. Rooster's making fish chowder for everyone tonight."

"Good for Rooster," I said, grimacing at the thought. "Is Chef Claire already at the restaurant?"

"She is. Josie should be here soon. Said she was coming up for lunch."

I nodded and glanced around the living room. I mentally added dusting and vacuuming to my to-do list. Then I exhaled loudly and sighed.

"What's wrong, darling?"

"Selma Blankenship was killed last night," I said as a simple statement of fact.

"What?" my mother said, reacting enough to cause Max to stir. We waited it out and Max eventually dozed back off. "What on earth happened?"

"It looks like she was smothered in her sleep," I said.

"Oh, the poor woman," she said, frowning.

"But don't worry about having to change today's program. Dianne is still going to speak at two."

"She is?" my mother said, raising an eyebrow. "Interesting."

"Yeah, I thought so too," I said, then noticed Max staring at me. "Well, look who's finally awake."

I got up and lifted her off my mother's chest and held her close. Max waved her arms and kicked her legs.

"Somebody's excited to see you," my mother said, sitting up on the couch and stretching her arms over her head. "It's your Mama."

"Hey, Sweetie," I said, rocking her gently in my arms. Then I heard the kitchen door open and Josie appeared moments later. "Hey. How are things down at the Inn?"

"Busy, but good," Josie said, gently stroking the back of Max's head. "I managed to front load my schedule so I can go to Dianne's presentation."

81

"It should be memorable," I said.

"How was fishing?" Josie said.

"Cut short by a murder," I said.

"What?"

"Selma Blankenship was killed in her hotel room last night."

"Geez. I knew it had been too quiet around here lately. Any idea who did it?"

"Not yet," I said.

"My money is on the Kneeler," Josie said.

"She's probably a good a place to start," I said with a shrug.

"What sort of motive could she have had?" my mother said.

"Too soon to tell," I said. "One big question needs to be answered before we can begin to figure that out."

"It's too early in the day for cryptic, Suzy," Josie said. "Enlighten me, oh, wise one."

"Who the intended victim was," I said.

"Yeah, that is a good question," Josie said, nodding. "Definitely a great place to start."

"Nothing gets past you."

Chapter 8

I glanced around the packed auditorium where several hundred people were chatting in hushed voices as we waited for the presentation to begin. Their conversations created a noisy buzz in the room, and I did my best to ignore it as I continued my surveillance.

"So, let me get this straight," Josie whispered as she leaned in close. "Selma and Dianne switched rooms yesterday."

"Yes."

"Before or after their meeting in the afternoon?"

"I'm not sure. Yet."

She snorted, drawing the attention of several people sitting nearby. She glanced around and shrugged at the stares. "Sorry. My allergies are acting up."

"Smooth," I said, laughing. "I'm going to chat with the Chief and Detective Williams later. They must have some more details put together by now." I spotted Claudia sitting by herself in the front row. "She doesn't look well."

"How can you tell?" Josie said, following my eyes. "I'm surprised she's actually sitting in a chair."

"Dianne fired her yesterday," I said. "If she was the intended victim, I smell a motive."

"I smell popcorn," Josie said, glancing around. "Did we miss that on our way in?"

"You just had lunch," I said, staring at her.

"I know," she said, scanning the back of the room for signs of a popcorn vendor. "But this is kinda like going to the movies."

"Unbelievable."

"That's okay," she said, digging through her bag. "I came prepared."

"Ooh," I said, spotting what was in the plastic bag now sitting on her lap. "Chef Claire made brownies?"

"She did," Josie said, holding the bag out to me.

I took one of the brownies and broke a piece off. I popped it into my mouth just as I spotted Joshua Jenkins sit down next to Claudia. I mumbled through the half-chewed brownie and Josie stared at me.

"What? Try it again without a mouthful of walnuts."

I swallowed, cleared my throat then repeated myself.

"I said look who's sitting with Claudia."

"Well, she is his agent, right?"

84

"She is," I said, nodding as I watched their whispered conversation play out. "I wonder how Joshua is handling Claudia's behavior these days."

"She represents two pretty famous authors," Josie said. "Well, one now. She must have some skills, right?"

With no answer to the question, I shrugged as I focused on the rest of Dianne's travel party. Wilbur Smithers, the lawyer, was sitting quietly listening to something Imelda, Selma's former assistant, was telling him. Eventually, he nodded and casually draped an arm around the back of her chair. As he extended his arm, his hand gently brushed the back of the woman's head. I glanced at Josie who was closely watching the interplay between the couple.

"Was that a casual move or did he mean to touch her?" I said.

"Hard to tell," she said. "But I think that might have been the point. If they are an item, they're certainly doing everything they can not to show it."

"Yeah," I said. "If it's a workplace romance, they probably want to keep it quiet. I need to talk to them."

"Now, there's a surprise," she said, making quick work of her brownie.

"Imelda was Selma's personal assistant. And Wilbur is Blankenship's lead counsel."

"So?"

"So, that means they probably spent more time with Selma than anyone else," I said. "Whatever is going on at the company, those two have to be in the loop. And since Dianne was doing everything she could to get out from under her contract, there has to be-"

"Suzy?"

"Yeah."

"Eat your brownie."

I made a face at her but complied and sat quietly as I worked my way through the rest of my snack. A few minutes later, Dianne walked onto the stage to enormous applause. She smiled, took a small bow then approached the podium.

"She looks stressed," I said, carefully studying her face and hand gestures.

"I'd be stressed too," Josie said. "Either somebody is trying to kill her, or she's worried about being charged with Selma's murder."

"She didn't do it," I snapped as I glared at Josie.

I received several stares from the people sitting around us. I also got shushed by the couple sitting on Josie's right.

86

"Sorry," I whispered.

"I should hope so," the couple said in unison as they continued to stare at me.

"Okay, Fan Girl, dial it down a notch," she said, then reached into her pocket. "Here, have a brownie," Josie said, handing the plastic bag to them without making eye contact.

The couple stared at the bag then shrugged and accepted it. They sat quietly, hunched over as they surreptitiously began eating.

Dianne began with a reading from her latest book, one I'd read about a year ago. Then she seamlessly transitioned into a presentation that outlined her writing process. I listened closely and nodded along with her as she made various points.

"She's a total pro," I whispered.

"She is," Josie said, without taking her eyes off the author. "I have no idea how she's managing to come off so cool and collected after what happened."

"That's what pros do."

"I guess," Josie said. "All I know is that I couldn't do it after a morning like she had."

Her comment stuck with me and nagged as Dianne continued. Fifteen minutes later, she finished her presentation to loud applause then took questions from the audience. She glanced around at dozens of hands in the air then pointed at someone in the back of the room. A young man, carrying a microphone, dashed up the aisle and handed it to the questioner.

"Thank you so much for being here, Ms. Harman," he said. "But could you answer the question that's on all our minds? When will you be releasing a new book?"

"Hopefully, it won't be long," Dianne said tentatively through a small smile.

"Are you dealing with writer's block?" the man said.

"No, I'm writing all the time," she said. "And I think you'll soon see that I've been very busy the past year."

"I'm glad to hear that," the man said, turning slightly to the side to prevent the young man from taking the microphone back. "Just one more question. Do you think the murder last night of your publisher will speed up or slow down the release of your new book?"

"Whoa," Josie said, craning her neck to identify the man asking the questions. "Do you know that guy?"

"I do not," I said as a loud murmur continued to build and rumble around the room. "I guess most people hadn't heard about Selma's death."

"Well, they have now," Josie said, still studying the questioner closely. "He's leaving."

"Throw a nasty question then get the heck out of Dodge," I said, watching the man depart through the door. "I need to have a chat with that guy."

"Well, you're going to have to wait," she said, settling back into her seat.

I nodded and focused on Dianne who was obviously trying to figure out how to respond to the question. Eventually, she approached the microphone and scanned the audience before continuing.

"Yes, I'm afraid that tragic news is true," she said softly. "My publisher, Selma Blankenship, did die last evening. We're waiting for the police to give us more details."

The crowd murmured again and Dianne waited it out. When a semblance of silence returned, she leaned in close to the microphone.

"Next question, please."

Claudia's hand immediately shot up from the front row. Dianne couldn't miss the energetic wave that resembled a third grader who was sure she knew the answer. Dianne eventually nodded at her former agent.

"Yes, Claudia. What's your question?"

"Rumor has it you're currently in the middle of a dispute to terminate your contract with Blankenship Publishing. Is that true?"

"What a little snot," Josie said, glaring at the back of the agent's head.

"Yeah, that was a cheap shot," I said.

"Yes, Claudia," Dianne said softly. "As I'm sure you know, I am currently in discussions with my publisher to modify my business relationship with them."

"It's interesting that Selma died right in the middle of those discussions, wouldn't you say?" Claudia said, her sarcasm impossible to miss.

"I think the appropriate term for what happened to Selma is tragic, Claudia," Dianne said, doing her best to remain calm. "Next question, please."

My hand shot up and Dianne spotted it immediately.

"Yes, Suzy," she said. "What's your question?"

"Could you talk a bit more about where your ideas come from?"

"I'd be happy to," Dianne said, relaxing a bit.

"Well done," Josie said, patting my knee.

"Thanks," I whispered, then listened to the author's response.

Fifteen minutes later, without receiving any more references to Selma's death, Dianne informed the crowd she'd be in the lobby for a meet and greet and was happy to sign books. She finished to loud applause and left the stage. The crowd filed out and made a beeline for the area where the signing was being held. Josie and I remained in our seats as the room emptied. Wilbur and Imelda strolled past and waved as they continued their hushed conversation. Joshua Jenkins walked by and stopped in his tracks when he saw us.

"It looked like things were going to go off the rails for a while there," he said. "Good job getting us back on track."

"Thanks," I said. "What the hell is wrong with Claudia?"

"She's pissed," he said with a shrug. "Don't forget to stop by my booth later. I'll be signing all afternoon."

He wandered off with a small, trailing wave. Josie watched him go then shook her head.

"He's a bit too casual about the whole thing, wouldn't you say?"

"Yeah," I said, nodding. "But he is totally self-absorbed. That might explain it."

"What sort of motive could he have?"

"As far as Dianne goes, I don't have a clue," I said, waving to a local couple I was good friends with. "But if Selma was the intended victim, maybe he was fighting with her as well."

"It sure didn't sound like it at dinner last night," Josie said. "He was sucking up to Selma all night."

"Maybe Selma was thinking about dropping him," I said. "The lawyer did take some shots at Joshua about his recent sales."

"He did," Josie said. "Do you think Joshua might have done it?"

"I think we need to figure out who the target was before we can make any assumptions about who the killer was," I said.

"Oh, I hate when that happens," Josie deadpanned.

I laughed and gently punched her on the shoulder.

"Okay, what now?" she said, getting to her feet.

"I'm going to have a chat with the Chief and Detective Williams," I said, glancing around the almost empty auditorium. "If I can find them."

"I hear a sausage and pepper sandwich calling my name," she said. "Do you need to get home and relieve your mom and Paulie?"

"No, they cleared their schedule for the weekend," I said. "She wants me to have some time to myself. Says I need a bit of a break."

"She's a great Grandma."

"She is," I said, then laughed. "And it gives her a chance to start spoiling Max without any interference."

"The kid's four months old," Josie said. "How spoiled can she get at that age?"

"We're gonna find out," I said, then an idea floated to the surface. "I think we should invite everyone to C's tonight."

"Dianne's group?"

"Yeah," I said. "Maybe one or more will feel the need to unburden themselves after a great meal and several bottles of wine."

"Ah, an oldie but a goodie," Josie said. "Okay, I'll see you later. What time do you want to meet at the restaurant?"

"Let's shoot for seven," I said, glancing at my watch. "You mind giving the restaurant a call and making the reservation?"

"No problem. Your mom's table?"

"Yeah, she won't be using it tonight."

"Just try to behave yourself," Josie said.

"Don't I always?"

Josie raised an eyebrow at me then shook her head and headed up the aisle. I stood next to my chair, alone with my thoughts. I made a quick mental checklist of what I needed to do before dinner, then headed backstage to see how my new friend was holding up.

Chapter 9

After extending the dinner invitation to the still shaken Dianne, I headed outside and felt the blast of a hot, sticky August afternoon. I hadn't had a chance to tour the various Festival booths, so I slowly meandered my way through the downtown streets that had been converted into a carnival atmosphere.

I stopped at one booth that featured ornate stained-glass lamps and bought one for my mom as a thank you gift for taking such good care of Max. After that, it took me a half-hour to walk a hundred feet when I crossed paths with several friends I hadn't seen much of since the baby was born. I happily answered all their questions, and by the time I finished, my mood had brightened.

I spotted the Chief and Detective Williams standing off to one side of a food truck selling barbecued chicken. They were eating and doing their best not to make a mess of themselves in the process. They were failing miserably.

"Hey," the Chief mumbled through a mouthful of food. "Great turnout."

"It is," I said, taking another look around the crowded streets. I paused when a whiff of grilling chicken wafted over me. My stomach rumbled but I shook it off and maintained my focus. "Did you get a chance to listen to Dianne's presentation?"

"No, we've been busy," Detective Williams said. "Anything interesting happen?"

"One of the questioners grilled Dianne pretty hard," I said. "He spilled the beans to several hundred people about Selma's murder."

"Who was it?" the Chief said, wiping his mouth.

"No idea," I said. "But he seemed strange. And then Claudia, the agent Dianne just fired, put her on the spot with a nasty question."

The cops glanced back and forth at each other.

"What is it?" I said, unable to miss their reaction.

"Agent Tompkins came through," the Chief said.

"Already?" I said, surprised by the news.

"Hey, somebody might have just tried to kill his favorite aunt," the Chief said. "He dropped everything else he was working on after we talked to him."

"He's got some information about Claudia?"

"He's got information on all of them," Detective Williams said.

"Well, I can't wait to hear it," I said, rocking back and forth on my heels.

"If you can wait a while," the Chief said. "You'll be able to hear it from the horse's mouth."

"He's coming up?"

"He flew by helicopter to a military airfield, then caught a private jet to Buffalo. He's driving in from there. He should be here in a couple of hours," Detective Williams said, polishing off the last of his chicken.

"I guess it pays to be a senior FBI official, huh?" I said.

"It can't hurt," Detective Williams said, then spotted a splotch of barbecue sauce on his shirt. "Dang it. I knew I couldn't get through that without spilling."

"Try taking human bites," I deadpanned with a grin.

"I'll try to remember that," the detective said. "We're going to debrief with him when he gets here."

"Can I come?"

The cops looked at each other then Detective Williams nodded.

"Actually, we were planning on inviting you."

"You were? Since when?" I said, raising an eyebrow as I glanced back and forth at them.

97

"Since you're spending so much time with the author," Detective Williams said. "Who knows what she might say, right?"

"She didn't do it," I said. "And if you know what's good for you, you might want to keep your suspicions about Dianne to yourself when her nephew gets here."

"Agent Tompkins already knows she's a suspect," the Chief said.

"What?"

"Why do you think he dropped everything to get up here?" Detective Williams said.

"She didn't do it," I repeated. "In fact, we're not even sure if she wasn't the intended victim."

"Let's just say we're considering all our options at the moment and leave it at that," the detective said, finally giving up on getting the stain out of his shirt.

"Fine," I said, annoyed by his tone. "But if you float that theory, you'll be the one who ends up with egg on his face."

"I'm not worried about eggs," the detective said as he glanced down at the stain on his shirt. "Right now, I'm trying to deal with barbecued chicken."

"Funny," I said, making a face at him. "What time is he getting here?"

"Around six," the Chief said.

"Perfect. He'll be able to join us for dinner."

"Dinner?" the Chief said.

"I'm inviting Dianne and her group to dinner at C's," I said. "I'd invite you, but I doubt if the presence of the two cops investigating the murder will help the conversation."

"But you want to invite an FBI agent?" Detective Williams said.

"No, I'm not inviting an FBI agent," I said with an impish grin. "I'm inviting the concerned nephew."

Chapter 10

I drove home to check on Max and shower before dinner. But before I headed up to the house, I stopped by the Inn where I spotted Sammy and Jill, along with Josie and Lacie, our new vet, fawning over a large cardboard box sitting on top of the registration desk.

"What do we have here?" I said as I approached.

"Take a look," Josie said.

I peered over the edge and saw a mass of black and brown fur. The puppies were huddled together and sleepily doing their best to get comfortable. I reached into the box to stroke all their heads then glanced around at the others.

"There are six of them," Sammy said. "Henrietta Clemons found them in her barn and brought them in."

"Any sign of the mother?" I said, glancing down into the box.

"No," Sammy said. "Henrietta said a stray cocker-mix of some sort had been hanging around her place. But she hasn't seen her in a couple of days."

"What sort of shape are they in?" I said, glancing back and forth at Josie and Lacie.

"A little malnourished," Lacie said. "But other than that, I think they're going to be okay. We were just about to take a closer look."

"How old do you think they are?" I said, lifting one of the puppies out of the box and nestling it against my chest.

"Around a month," Josie said. "Sammy, let's set up a feeding schedule for them."

"Bottle feeding?" Sammy said softly as he glanced at Jill.

I understood Sammy's trepidation. Dealing with bottle feeding a litter of pups was an arduous task that required a lot of the staff's time. But Sammy, like the rest of our staff, willingly did whatever was required to make sure our residents were healthy and safe.

"No, let's try easing them into solid food," Josie said, then turned to Lacie. "What do you think?"

"Yeah, let's start with that," Lacie said. "We can always go back to just milk if their little tummies can't handle it."

"Mix that high protein puppy formula with some warm milk," Josie said to Sammy. "Make sure it's got that thin gruel consistency before you give it to them."

"Got it," Sammy said, nodding. "Four times a day?"

"Yeah," Josie said, reaching into the box to pet the puppies. "For now, let's start with a bath. You guys stink."

Sammy lifted the box and, trailed by Jill and Lacie, headed for the back of the Inn. Josie watched them depart then turned to me.

"Any update?"

"Agent Tompkins is on his way up," I said. "He'll be joining us for dinner."

"Does Chef Claire know yet?" Josie said.

"Not yet," I said. "It's too bad the restaurant is so busy. I doubt she's going to have much time to socialize. And he'll be busy trying to clear his aunt's name from murder charges."

"The cops don't really think that nice woman actually killed her, do they?" Josie said with a frown.

"I don't think so. But you know Detective Williams. Until he's convinced, she's stays on the list."

"I still like the Kneeler for it."

"That would be too easy, right?"

"Any woman who organizes her ziti before she eats it is capable of anything."

"There is that," I said. "I'm heading up to the house. You ready to go?"

"Yeah, I'm done down here."

We headed for the back of the Inn and spent the next fifteen minutes saying hello to all the dogs before leaving. I huffed and puffed my way up the steps that led to the house. Josie noticed my labored breathing and stared at me.

"I know," I said. "I thought Max would be all I needed to get back in decent shape."

"But?"

"But I was wrong," I said, laughing.

"Get serious about Chef Claire's offer to put together a training program for you."

"That's all I need," I said, frowning. "Start doing exercise with her. She'd wear me down to a nub."

"No pain, no gain," Josie said as she climbed the back steps two at a time.

"Showoff," I said, one hand clutching the railing as I followed her.

We entered the kitchen and were greeted by all four house dogs. Then I heard Max wailing and headed straight for the living room where my mom was gently bouncing my daughter against her chest.

"She's been like this since she woke up," my mother said. "Haven't you, Max?"

Max answered the question by turning up the volume of her howls. I reached out and took her from my mother.

103

Immediately, her cries began to soften. Soon, she was nestled contentedly against me. My mother smiled at me.

"She just missed her mama," my mother said, sitting down on the couch.

"I think it's the first time she's woken up without me being here," I said, frowning. "I can't believe I wasn't here."

"Darling, if that's the biggest moment you ever miss in your daughter's life, count your blessings."

"Yeah, I suppose," I said, giving her comment some thought.

"And you did the same thing," she said. "You always woke up cranky." She motioned for me to sit down then joined me on the couch. "But now, you're always an absolute delight in the morning," she deadpanned.

"Funny."

"You're doing a wonderful job with her, darling."

"Thanks, Mom."

"Do you have any update?" she said, smiling at Max who was already dozing off.

"Not much yet," I said. "I should know more after Agent Tompkins gets here."

My mother nodded then yawned and stretched.

"For now, they still have Dianne on their list of suspects. I don't get it. There's no way she could have done it."

"Darling, if there's one thing all your adventures should have taught you by now it's that people are capable of anything."

I couldn't argue the point.

Chapter 11

I arrived at the police station at 6:30 sharp and found all three men sitting around the Chief's desk chatting quietly. I greeted Agent Tompkins with a hug then sat down.

"What did I miss?"

"Nothing. We just got here," Chief Abrams said, then focused on the FBI agent. "You got anything useful?"

"I guess we'll see," Agent Tompkins said, removing his phone from his pocket. "Normally, I'd have all this written down in a report. But the updates have been coming in all day. So, I may be jumping around a bit."

"Not a problem," the Chief said as he leaned back in his chair and put his feet up on the desk.

"Comfy?" I deadpanned.

"Not as comfortable as I'd be on my couch," he said. "But duty calls, right?"

"How do you want to do this?" Agent Tompkins said, scrolling through his phone.

106

"I'd start with the victim," I said to no one in particular. Then I caught the looks all three were giving me. Mildly embarrassed, I shrugged. "But that's just me."

"It's as good a place as any," Agent Tompkins said. "Okay, Selma Blankenship, owner, CEO, and Chairwoman of Blankenship Publishing. Just short of her fiftieth birthday, divorced with no kids, lived in Connecticut."

"She drove into the City to work?" Detective Tompkins said.

"She was driven," Agent Tompkins said. "She was picked up at her house every morning, Monday to Saturday, at 5:30."

"Early riser," the Chief said. "How long had she owned the company?"

"Let's see," Agent Tompkins said, scrolling through his phone. "Almost fifteen years. The company struggled the first few years then took off."

"When she signed Dianne, right?" I said.

"Yes, among other mystery writers," Agent Tompkins said. "I remember when that happened. Aunt Dianne was so excited."

"She's been with Blankenship a long time," Detective Williams said.

"She has," Agent Tompkins said. "And they both made each other a lot of money. But when the internet and online buying exploded, Blankenship, like a lot of other publishing outfits, wasn't prepared for the revolution."

"Revolution?" Chief Abrams said.

"It's really not too strong of a word," Agent Tompkins said. "Total disruption to the business model."

"But Blankenship has been able to survive," I said.

"They have," Agent Tompkins said. "According to my folks, Blankenship had gotten fat and sloppy over the years, and when the industry started its slide, the company was forced to cut way back. They moved offices to save money, let a whole bunch of staff and underperforming authors go, then basically held on for dear life. She talked with a couple of companies looking to acquire Blankenship, but she turned them all down."

"The offer wasn't big enough?" Detective Williams said.

"I think it was more about loss of control over day to day operations," Agent Tompkins said. "Selma was a bit of a control freak."

"How bad did it get?" I said.

"Bad enough to file bankruptcy about six years ago," Agent Tompkins said. "But they dug out and actually

108

turned a decent profit the past couple of years. Nothing like they used to make, but not bad."

"And then Dianne told Selma she was leaving," I said.

"Pretty much," Agent Tompkins said. "Aunt Dianne showed me the numbers, and it makes a lot of sense from a business standpoint to go indie. Not to mention the fact she'll have total control over her work."

"How much damage to the company would her leaving create?" Detective Williams said.

"Nothing fatal, but enough to hurt," Agent Tompkins said. "But I think Blankenship was more worried about the precedent it might set. Aunt Dianne has a lot of clout with other authors. I'm sure Selma was worried others might follow her lead."

"Makes sense," I said. "Did you know she was fighting with Blankenship?"

"Aunt Dianne mentioned she was planning to leave, but she never went into much detail. Until twenty minutes ago, that is." Then he reached into the pocket of his jacket. "I almost forgot." He tossed a small evidence bag on the desk. Inside was a piece of plastic the size of a credit card. "I thought you guys might want this."

"What is it?" Detective Williams said as he examined the object.

"The key to Selma's suite. Aunt Dianne found it in her purse."

"She didn't turn it in when they changed rooms?" I said.

"She thought she did," Agent Tompkins said with a shrug. "And she was genuinely surprised when she found it."

"Interesting," Detective Williams said.

"How so?" Agent Tompkins said, immediately on guard.

"She had the key to the room of a woman she was doing battle with. Someone who was making her life miserable," Detective Williams said.

The FBI agent's eyes narrowed and he stared at the state cop. I sat back in my chair and glanced back at forth at both men as the tension in the room ramped up.

"And your point is?" Agent Tompkins said.

"My point is that your aunt appears to have had both motive and opportunity," Detective Williams said, not backing down from the agent's withering stare.

"She didn't do it," I said.

"You don't know that, Suzy," Detective Williams said. "Think it through. A successful author with a ton of fans who think she walks on water. Someone who wants to make a major change but is being thwarted at every step by her publishing company. I know I'd be cranky. Not to mention the fact she spends all her time thinking up creative ways to kill people in her books."

"That's my aunt you're talking about," Agent Tompkins said, almost coming out of his chair.

"I'm talking about a murder suspect," Detective Williams said. "If anybody should know that you don't take this stuff personally, it's you, *Agent* Tompkins."

"Okay, guys," the Chief said, removing his feet from the desk and leaning forward in his chair. "How about we dial it down a couple of notches?"

Both of them nodded but continued to glare at each other.

"Did Dianne tell you about Blankenship's problems when you talked with her today?" I said.

"No," Agent Tompkins said, finally softening his glare. "It was all in the file."

"You have a file on Selma?" I said, frowning.

"No, we have a file on Wilbur Smithers," the agent said.

"The lawyer?" I said.

"Oh, he's a lot more than just a lawyer," Agent Tompkins said, again scrolling through his messages.

111

"Wilbur Smithers has been on our radar for several years. Or he was before he landed at Blankenship."

"What's he been up to?" the Chief said.

"Racketeering. Money laundering. And a host of other delightful white-collar crimes," the agent said.

"Arrested and charged?" the Chief said.

"No," the agent said, shaking his head.

"OC?" Detective Williams said.

"Yeah, we're sure he's mobbed up," Agent Tompkins said. "Or at least he was. When things headed south for OC in New York, he got out while the getting was good."

"And landed at a publishing company?" I said, confused.

"Eventually, yeah. I thought it was odd, too," the agent said. "According to my guys, he built his reputation as a turnaround guy. A classic fixer who's good with money and knows how to make deals. And how to make problems go away."

"Problems like your aunt?" I said, raising an eyebrow.

"The thought has crossed my mind," he said.

"So, Smithers is a brains over muscle kind of guy?" I said.

"Exactly," Agent Tompkins said. "But he certainly knows how to use muscle when necessary."

"But why would Blankenship want to kill your aunt?" Detective Williams said. "Wouldn't that be like killing off the golden goose?"

"A golden goose who was about to take all her eggs elsewhere," I said.

"I can make it work," the Chief said. "If Blankenship couldn't have her, nobody could."

"No, I don't see it," Detective Williams said. "There would be other ways to do serious damage without killing her. Like trashing her in the media. Doing everything they could to ruin her reputation."

"You're right," Agent Tompkins said.

I sat quietly with my neurons surging. Then a question floated to the surface.

"Who else knew about the room change?"

"Aunt Dianne isn't sure. Obviously, Selma knew. But she doesn't know if she told anyone else."

"How is she holding up?" I said.

"She's pretty rattled, but she'll be fine," Agent Tompkins said. "She's tough as nails when she needs to be." He caught the look on Detective William's face. "You got something to say?"

"Not at the moment," the detective said.

"She mentioned some guy who referenced Selma's death during the Q&A this afternoon," Agent Tompkins said.

"Yeah, there was," I said. "I didn't recognize him and didn't see him after the presentation."

"You got anything on the rest of the group?" the Chief said.

"I do," the agent said. "That's the good thing about having a file open on somebody. You usually end up with a lot of information on the other people he's in contact with."

"Lovely," I said, again coming face to face with the realization of how much information the government must have on all of us. "I'd love to see the file you guys have got on me."

"No, you wouldn't," the agent deadpanned.

"What?"

"I'm joking, Suzy," he said, laughing. "We don't have a file on you. But I'd be happy to open one."

"Thanks, but I think I'll pass," I said, making a face at him. "What's the deal with Claudia?"

"Claudia," Agent Tompkins said, shaking his head. "She's a piece of work."

"You know her?" the Chief said.

"Sure, I know Claudia very well," the agent said. "I've been to several events Aunt Dianne has done over the years. And we always try to go to dinner whenever she's in town on a book tour. Claudia is always by her side."

"Did she tell you she fired Claudia yesterday?" I said.

"It's about time," Agent Tompkins said. "But if there's one thing my aunt is, it's loyal."

"But her screwing up the contract was the last straw?" I said.

"Among other things," the agent said.

"What contract screw up?" Detective Williams said.

"Apparently, there's some language in the contract that is unclear. And that's been making it hard for Dianne to walk away," I said.

"When did you plan on telling us that little nugget?" Detective Williams said.

"Right now?" I deadpanned.

"Funny. You should have mentioned it," the detective said, obviously miffed with me.

But it wasn't the first time, and I seriously doubted if it would be the last.

"I'm sorry, Detective Williams," I said. "But in case you haven't noticed, there's been a lot going on today."

"Suzy," the Chief said, his voice rising a notch. "Easy."

"Yeah. Sorry, Detective Williams. It just slipped my mind." I focused on the FBI agent. "What does Claudia's history look like?"

"It reads like a textbook example of clinical psychoses," he said. "Over the years, she was in and out of institutions until they finally got her meds right."

"She's on medication?" Detective Williams said.

"Nothing gets past you," Agent Tompkins said, then winked at me.

"Well played, Agent Tompkins," I said, laughing.

Detective Williams didn't find it as funny and sat tight-lipped as he waited for the agent to continue.

"She's on quite a chemical cocktail," Agent Tompkins said.

"That's in the file?" the Chief said.

"No, I got that from my aunt," the agent said. "And I've witnessed Claudia's behavior firsthand over the years."

"Why did your aunt fire her?" Detective Williams said.

"Basically, my aunt doesn't need her. And I think she finally got worn down carrying her. You know, always having to clean up her messes."

"She is odd," I said.

116

"Claudia a long way from odd," the agent said. "Have you had the pleasure of dining with her yet?"

"Twice," I said, nodding. "We had lunch then I invited Dianne and her group to dinner at the house last night."

"Lucky you," Agent Tompkins said, laughing. "I hope you put her on the left corner of the table."

"After what we saw at lunch, we did," I said.

I caught the looks the Chief and Detective Williams were giving both of us.

"She's left-handed," I said by way of explanation.

"Thanks for clearing that up," Detective Williams said.

"She has this thing about sitting on the end of the table," Agent Tompkins said. "Did she eat dinner standing up?"

"No, she was kneeling on a footstool," I said.

"She must be going through one of her religious phases. When she gets overloaded with stress, she tends to gravitate to heavenly powers," he said.

"Do you think she could have tried to kill your aunt?" the Chief said.

"Before today, I would have said there wasn't a chance in hell she'd be capable of doing that. But getting fired is going to turn her world, what's left of it, upside down."

"So, you do think it's possible she tried to kill her?" Detective Williams said.

"I'd have to see her before I could make that judgment," Agent Tompkins said. "But if anybody could manage to screw up and kill the wrong person, it would be Claudia."

"What do you know about Selma's assistant?" the Chief said.

"Imelda?" Agent Tompkins said. "There's not much in the file about her. Most of what I know is pretty much gossip my aunt has told me."

"Here comes the juicy part," I said with a grin as I leaned forward.

"Yeah, actually it's not bad," the agent said, laughing. "According to my aunt, Imelda has struck up a rather intense personal relationship with our friend, Wilbur Smithers."

"The lawyer and Imelda," I said, nodding. "Interesting. I thought I picked something up between those two."

"You were right," Agent Tompkins said. "Apparently, when the rumors began to surface, it didn't sit well with Imelda's former lover. It created a lot of tension around the office."

118

"Let me guess, she was sleeping with one of Blankenship's authors," Detective Williams said.

"No," Agent Tompkins said, turning coy.

We sat in silence then the lightbulb went off.

"Selma?" I whispered.

"You're good," Agent Tompkins said, staring at me.

"Thanks. I have my moments," I said, pondering the implications of what I'd just learned.

"Selma and Imelda were at war over it?" the Chief said.

"Well, it definitely had an impact on their work relationship," Agent Tompkins said. "Not to mention the other stuff. But the real hostility was between Wilbur and Selma."

"Because he stole her girlfriend?" Detective Williams said.

"That's how Selma saw it," the agent said.

"You got all that from your aunt?" the detective said. "I mean, it wasn't in the file, right?"

"No. But it is now," Agent Tompkins said with a shrug.

"What about Joshua Jenkins?" I said.

"He seems to be a loner," Agent Tompkins said. "Lives way out in the wilderness in Montana and just wants to be left alone to write his books. Hates doing book tours and signings. Decent guy, but nondescript."

"Probably not much there," the Chief said.

"Unless you consider the fact that Selma was in the process of dropping him. His sales have been slipping for a while. And according to Aunt Dianne, Wilbur was adamant his contract wasn't going to be renewed."

"The lawyer got that big of a vote?" Detective Williams said.

"He did. I suppose he still will. Maybe even a bigger one," Agent Tompkins said.

"I have a question," I said.

"Only one. Stop the presses," the Chief said.

"Funny," I said, then focused on the FBI agent. "Now that Selma is dead, who gets control of Blankenship?"

"Great minds think alike," he said. "I've been asking myself that question since this morning."

Chapter 12

Dinner started with a bang when Claudia arrived at the table, looked down at the empty chair in front of her then stared off into space with a befuddled look on her face. Everyone did their best to ignore her, but she continued to stand dead still, unsure of her next move. Josie looked up from her menu and glanced down the table at me before focusing on the woman who was now repeatedly running her hands through her hair.

"Sorry, Claudia," Josie said. "All our footstools are in the shop."

"What?" Claudia said, turning to Josie, her confusion ramped up a notch.

"Yes," I said, flashing Josie a dirty look before coming to the rescue. "We're in the process of getting them reupholstered."

"Please, Claudia," Dianne said softly. "Have a seat."

She reluctantly sat down and fiddled with her menu. I watched in silence then snuck a peek at Dianne who appeared to be taking several deep breaths.

121

"What's good here," Claudia said, her menu still unopen.

"All of it," I said. "You really can't make a bad choice."

"Don't bet on it," Wilbur Smithers said without looking up.

Imelda, sitting next to him, stifled a snort then took a sip of wine.

"Dianne tells me you're with the FBI," Wilbur said, focusing on Agent Tompkins.

"I am," he said.

"Where are you based out of?" the lawyer said.

"D.C."

"Headquarters," Wilbur said, nodding. "You're a long way from home. What brings you up here?"

"I thought I'd take advantage of Aunt Dianne's proximity. We don't get a chance to see each other very often."

"Proximity?" Wilbur said. "You need a guide dog to find this place."

"You should try finding it in the winter," Josie said.

"Thanks, but I'll pass," the lawyer said.

Dianne leaned over and whispered to Claudia who continued to have trouble getting settled in. Claudia listened closely then nodded and got up from the table.

"I'll be right back," she announced to no one in particular then headed off.

"What was that all about?" I whispered to Dianne.

"I asked if she'd remembered to take her meds," she said. "She hadn't."

"I suppose that's good news," I said. "I mean, she should be able to settle down after they kick in, right?"

"She should be," Dianne said. "As long as she doesn't drink too much wine."

I leaned in very close to her and kept my voice as low as possible.

"Do you think she could have been involved?"

"Claudia?" Dianne said. Then she gave my question some thought before shaking her head. "No, I don't."

"Are you sure? You just fired her. She must be angry."

"She rarely gets mad," Dianne said, reaching for her wine glass. "I wish she would. Usually, bad news makes her depressed and she tends to…shrink into herself. If that makes any sense."

"It does," I said, then glanced around the table. My eyes landed on Joshua Jenkins, and I decided the author was a safe place to start. "Joshua, tell us all about your new book."

Wilbur and Imelda glanced down the table at me and shook their heads in unison. But it was too late. Joshua wiped his mouth then tossed his napkin on the table and leaned forward with both elbows on the table. He looked around until he was sure he had everyone's attention then launched.

"Well, it's a fascinating story about a man who goes to his fortieth high school reunion."

"Nice setup," I said, nodding.

"Yes, I thought so too," he said. "While he's there, he reconnects with his former girlfriend who ends up getting murdered on the dance floor. And you'll never guess what song is playing when she's killed."

I gave it some thought before responding.

"Forty-year reunion. That would put it somewhere around the late seventies. I'm gonna go with *Stayin Alive*."

"How did you know that?" Joshua whispered, apparently crushed I'd figured it out.

"Lucky guess," I said, doing my best to play it down. "I like the choice. You know, the song is upbeat and all about moving forward in the face of challenges. And when you juxtapose it against her murder, it provides a nice counterpoint."

"Yes, that's what I was going for," Joshua said. "But it would have been nice if you'd read it first. It's supposed to be a mystery."

"It's just a frigging song, Joshua," Wilbur said.

"Let it go," Imelda said softly as she patted the lawyer's hand.

"What's the storyline?" I said.

"The main character is, at first, the major suspect," the author said.

"Sure, I get that," I said, nodding. "Maybe his former girlfriend unceremoniously dumped him in high school and the cops assume it was something he never got over. You know, lost love, a burning desire for revenge he kept stoked over all those years."

Wilbur and Imelda both burst into laughter. I glanced down the table at them then at Joshua who sat quietly fiddling with his napkin.

"What?" I said. "I got it right?"

"It's like you wrote the book blurb," Imelda said.

"How about that?" I said, glancing down at the table at Josie who was already shaking her head at me. I couldn't miss Joshua's discomfort and tossed him a softball question to get his spirits up. "It sounds fascinating. Please, tell me more."

"Well, the story really takes off from there," Joshua said as he reached for his wine. "The backstory of all his former classmates are dealt with, and the main character spends a lot of the book having flashbacks to all those pesky high school situations."

"Pesky is a word for it," Imelda said.

Joshua ignored her and turned to me.

"The book has an amazing hook at the end," Joshua said, then cocked his head as if daring me to keep going. "I don't suppose you'd like to hazard a guess at what that might be?"

Something about his tone annoyed me. All I was doing was trying to make chit-chat. And it wasn't my fault I'd gotten lucky with my first two guesses. So, I bore down and let my neurons work their magic.

"Well, I suppose the girlfriend might have dumped him for one of the cool kids in school. Probably a jock. Maybe the quarterback of the football team. But after they'd been married for a while, he let himself go to seed and she divorced him. And the reunion was the ex-husband's chance to kill her off and blame the old boyfriend in the process." I stopped, let my comments marinate for a minute before shaking my head. "Nah, that would be too obvious."

Out of the corner of my eye, I spotted Wilbur and Imelda biting their lips to control their laughter. Dianne stared down at the table and avoided eye contact.

"No way," I said, stunned. "That's it?"

"Yes," Joshua said. "It was the ex-husband."

"I'm so sorry, Joshua," I said. "Like I said, it was just a lucky guess."

The author continued to fiddle with his napkin and barely managed a small nod of his head. I felt terrible and caught Josie's eye who merely shrugged.

"Do you write?" Wilbur said.

"Me? No."

"You're obviously good with story," he said. "Maybe you should think about giving it a shot. We're always on the lookout for new talent."

"Absolutely," Imelda said. "Especially now."

Wilbur flinched and gently squeezed her hand.

"I mean, yes, we're always on the lookout," Imelda said, recovering quickly.

I glanced at Agent Tompkins who hadn't missed the short exchange. Then I spotted Claudia making her way back to the table. She came to a stop behind her chair, then

127

slid it into like she was playing a game of musical chairs. She took several deep breaths before glancing around the table.

"Sorry I took so long," she said. "What did I miss?"

"Joshua was just telling everyone about his new book," Wilbur said.

"Great book," Claudia said, nodding her head vigorously as she reached for a piece of bread. "And what a hook at the end. I never saw it coming."

"Claudia?"

"Yes, Joshua?"

"Please stop talking."

Chapter 13

After dinner, we adjourned to the lounge for drinks. While not as jammed as the dining room, the lounge was busy. Fortunately, a large group was called to their table, and we took their place on various couches and chairs. I offered to place the drink order and headed to the bar where Millie, our bar manager, was giving instructions to two other bartenders while trying to deal with the orders stacking up from the dining room.

"Next time your mother has a brainstorm for a big event, tell her to mind her own business," Millie said with a laugh as she wiped her hands on a towel.

"It's been non-stop in here for three days," I said, glancing around at the crowd. "We've barely seen Chef Claire."

"And we're booked solid the next two," she said. "What can I get you guys?"

I gave her the order and leaned against the bar. I spotted Dianne having a whispered conversation with Claudia who'd settled down when her meds had kicked in. Now, she had a vacant stare I was pretty sure was more from the wine she's downed during dinner than the medication.

"I'll have Sally bring these over," Millie said.

"You don't think I can make it back to the table without spilling?"

"Uh, no," she said, flashing me a quick grin.

"Funny," I said. "So, apart from being busy, things are going well?"

"They are," she said, then shot a quick glance at the man sitting alone at the end of the bar. "Apart from him."

I studied the man who was staring off into space then I recognized him as the guy who'd grilled Dianne during the Q&A session.

"What's the matter with him?"

"I don't even dare to hazard a guess," Millie said, shaking a mixed drink. "Trust me, that is one rock you do not want to look under."

"Interesting," I said, pursing my lips. "I'll see you later. Try not to work too hard."

"I don't like my chances," she said, expertly pouring two glasses of a milky green concoction.

"What the heck are those?"

"Green Lanterns," she said.

"What in them?" I said, staring at the glasses.

130

"Lots of booze and a ton of sugar," she said. "Vodka, coconut rum, blue curacao, melon liqueur, pineapple juice and Sprite. I think they're disgusting, but I only make the drinks, right?"

"It does sound disgusting," I said. "Later."

I made my way to the end of the bar and stood next to the man who continued to stare off into space. I took a step back to let someone get by me and purposely bumped the man's arm. It seemed to wake him from his coma and he looked over at me.

"I'm sorry," I said. "It's so crowded in here."

"Yeah."

"Have we met? You look familiar."

"No."

"I'm Suzy."

"Hiram."

"Hiram? I love that name. Hebrew origin, if I'm not mistaken. Are you Jewish?"

"No, my old man was a boozer," he said, then removed a couple of twenties from a stack of bills and slid them under his glass.

I watched him make his way through the crowd and disappear out the front door. I headed back to the group and sat down next to Josie.

"Was that the guy from Dianne's presentation?" she said.

"It was," I said.

"What did he have to say for himself?"

"Yeah. No. Hiram. My old man was a boozer," I deadpanned.

"Chatty," she said with a laugh.

"Yeah, I thought so too. But I didn't get the boozer reference."

"Hiram Walker," Josie said, draping a leg over her knee as she settled into the couch.

"Oh, right," I said. "It's a Canadian distillery. Imagine naming your kid after your favorite brand of booze."

"Could have been worse."

"How so?" I said.

"His old man could have loved to drink Zombies."

"Actually, that's probably a better name for him than Hiram."

"What the heck are those?" Josie said, staring at the overloaded tray of drinks our server was carrying.

"Green Lanterns."

"The choice of superheroes everywhere?"

"After a couple of those, I don't think you'd be doing anything heroic. Apart from trying not to puke your guts out in the parking lot."

"Who's drinking them?" Josie said, glancing around at our group.

"Claudia and Joshua," I said, nodding in their direction. They were sitting on another couch and chatting quietly with each other out of earshot.

"By the way, nice job of deflating him at dinner," Josie said. "Poor guy. I thought he was going to cry."

"I didn't mean to do that," I said, my voice rising a notch. "I was just trying to get the conversation rolling. But did you see the way Wilbur and Imelda reacted?"

"I did," she said, taking a sip of wine. "They didn't even try to hide their contempt for him."

"Maybe Selma was about to cut him loose," I said, still struggling to find a piece of the puzzle that would get me on track.

"It's certainly possible," Josie said. "I read one of his books a couple of years ago. Not to be cruel, but he's a bit of a hack."

"Yeah, he's no Dianne, that's for sure."

"So, where are your neurons taking you?" Josie whispered.

"Nowhere yet. We don't even know who the intended victim was," I said, rubbing my forehead.

"I still like the Kneeler for it," Josie said, nodding in Claudia's direction.

"It seems too easy," I said, also glancing over. "But she is odd. I'll give you that."

"Odd?" Josie said with a frown. "She's about three light-years away from odd." She set her half-full wine glass down and stood up. "I need to get some sleep. You ready to go?"

"No, I think I'm going to hang for a while," I said, reaching into my bag for my car keys. "You okay to drive?"

"Yeah, I'm fine," she said. "I only had two glasses of wine all night."

"Go ahead and take my car. I'll get a ride home."

"I'll see you in the morning."

She said her goodbyes then headed out the front door. I sat quietly for a few minutes, sipping wine. Then Dianne approached and sat down next to me.

"Thanks again for dinner," she said. "The food was amazing."

"Thanks. Chef Claire is a magician."

"I need to get going. I'm sure Velcro is waiting for me to take him for his night walk."

"Sure," I said. "What time is the panel tomorrow?"

"Two," Dianne said. "It should be interesting. I hope Joshua is able to recover by then."

"I feel bad about doing that," I said.

"Don't," she said. "He's been mailing it in for the last few years. Maybe it'll be the wakeup call he needs." She started to get up, then paused. "You feel like taking a walk? I've got a couple of ideas about the new series I'd like to run by you."

"Sounds great," I said, getting to my feet.

I said my goodbyes, ignored the dirty look Joshua was giving me, then followed Dianne outside. We made the short walk to her hotel, and I waited in the lobby while she went upstairs to get the Vizsla. I was sitting near the registration desk when George, the manager approached. He was a lifelong resident of Clay Bay and was now somewhere in his sixties. I couldn't remember a time when he hadn't worked there.

"Hey, Suzy," he said. "You're up late."

"Hi, George. I'm just waiting for somebody. How are you holding up?"

"You mean, how am I dealing with somebody getting killed in my most expensive suite during peak season?" he said, sitting down next to me.

"Yeah," I said. "It's always something, right?"

He chuckled as he waved to one of his staff walking past us.

"It's a lot of money to leave on the table," he said. "Oh, I almost forgot. Are you going to be seeing Chief Abrams?"

"Actually, we're getting together for breakfast tomorrow. Why?"

"One of my chambermaids found something in the room he might want," George said, getting up and heading behind the registration desk.

He soon returned holding a leather journal. He handed it to me and I fought the urge to immediately open it and begin reading. Instead, I slipped it into my bag.

"Where did the chambermaid find it?"

"It was in the closet," George said. "It was tucked inside a bath towel."

The elevator door opened and Dianne and Velcro stepped out. The dog was wagging her tail non-stop and headed in my direction. Dianne released the lock on the

136

retractable lead and Velcro put her paws up on my shoulders.

"Hey, Velcro," I said with a laugh as I rubbed the dog's head and ears. I glanced up at Dianne who was beaming at the dog. "Are you ready to go?"

"I think we better," she said. "Somebody needs to pee."

I stood up and said goodbye to George then followed Dianne outside. Velcro soon found a set of bushes and took care of business. We watched in silence until the dog finished then we began walking across the parking lot. When we reached the street, we headed away from the downtown area up a tree-lined street that had always been one of my favorites. Dianne kept the lead tight, but occasionally let the Vizsla roam a bit while still tethered.

"A lot of people don't think I should use a retractable lead like this," she said. "They think I should be using a shoulder harness to keep her from straining her neck. But Velcro rarely gets far enough away from me to worry about it."

"I use the same one with Chloe," I said. "Not that she needs to be on a lead very often."

"It's a beautiful night," Dianne said. "This is the best time of year to be here, right?"

"It's up there," I said. "But I love the fall, too."

"But not the winters?"

"I used to love them when I was a kid," I said. "Not so much anymore."

"And that's why you spend winter in the Cayman Islands?"

"Pretty much," I said. "I fought the idea for a long time. But my mother eventually wore me down."

"She does seem tenacious," Dianne said, laughing.

"That's a word for it. Tell me a bit about the new series."

"It will focus on a woman who runs a mobile dog grooming service," she said, keeping a close eye on the Vizsla who was exploring a patch of grass just off the sidewalk.

"Interesting," I said. "A mystery series on wheels."

"Exactly," she said. "I like the idea of the main character being able to move around."

"Maybe you could give her a storyline that takes her across the country," I said.

"Like what?" Dianne said, coming to a stop. Velcro noticed and immediately returned and sat down at her feet. "You don't miss a thing, do you?" She knelt down and rubbed the dog's head before focusing on me. "Tell me more."

"I don't know," I said with a shrug. "Maybe she's on some journey to find someone. An ex-boyfriend. Lost family member. And each book could deal with a specific murder investigation as she continues her journey."

"Something like The Fugitive," she said, nodding. "The search for the one-armed man."

"Yeah, something like that," I said. "It would open the series up. And you'd have an endless supply of different characters and geographic locations."

"That's a brilliant idea," she said, staring at me. "You want to write it with me?"

"What?"

"Why not? You're obviously good with storylines. And I have a feeling there's a writer lurking beneath the surface."

"I have a hard enough time writing a grocery list."

"You're being modest," she said. "But you don't have to answer right away. Give it some thought. Let it…what's the term Josie uses?"

"Marinate."

"Yes, just let it marinate for a while," she said, resuming the walk.

Then we spotted something in the middle of the street about a hundred feet away.

"What the heck is that?" I said.

"It looks like a garbage bag."

"We should probably move it," I said. "If there's anything in it, it could do some damage if somebody ran over it." I started to walk toward it, but Dianne placed a hand on my arm.

"I'll get it," she said, taking up the slack in the lead and handing me the plastic handle.

"Let me know if it's heavy," I said. "I'll give you a hand."

Velcro noticed Dianne walking away and quickly tightened the slack on the lead. The dog strained against it, but I gently pulled her back.

"Velcro, stay," I said firmly.

The dog settled down but continued to keep a close eye on Dianne's movements. I walked up the sidewalk until I was directly across from her.

"What is it?" I called out.

"It's a bag of garbage," she said, bending down.

Before I could respond, I heard the roar of an engine. Then I spotted the vehicle coming over the crest of the hill with its lights off. It was traveling at a high rate of speed and bearing down on the author who was now standing dumbfounded in the middle of the street.

"What the hell?" I whispered.

As the car continued to head straight for her, Velcro struggled mightily against the lead and tore the handle out of my hand. The dog made a mad dash into the street as the car got even closer. Then the dog launched herself into the air and shoved Dianne out of the way with her front paws. Dianne stumbled toward the other side of the street then tumbled over, ending up flat on her back.

Moments later, I heard a sickening thud when the car hit Velcro. I watched in horror as the dog rolled over and over and eventually came to a stop next to a storm drain. The car continued without slowing and soon disappeared from sight. Dianne climbed to her feet and we both sprinted toward the dog who was whelping and having a hard time breathing.

"Oh, no," Dianne whispered as she started to tremble. "Velcro."

"Don't touch her," I said, reaching for my phone. "But talk to her. Try to keep her calm." I placed the call and waited impatiently. "C'mon. Pick up. C'mon, answer."

"Hey, what's up?" a very sleepy Josie said.

"Velcro just got hit by a car."

"Is she okay?"

"She's alive, but it looks like she's in bad shape."

"Where are you?"

"Just below the crest of the hill at Church and Major," I said, my vision blurred from the tears streaming down my face.

"I'm on my way."

"Call Sammy and Jill and have them meet us at the Inn. You're going to need some help."

Chapter 14

I headed into the street where Dianne was kneeling down over Velcro. The dog was having difficulty breathing and her eyes were wide open and glazed over. Dianne gently reached a hand out to pet the dog's head, and I called out to her in warning. But it was too late. The dog, obviously in shock, snapped at her and sunk its teeth deep into her hand. She snatched her hand back and stared at the blood streaming down her arm.

"Are you okay?" I said, reaching into my bag for a handful of tissues.

"I'll be fine," she said, bawling like a baby. "I can't believe she bit me."

I was certain she was crying from the accident as opposed to the fact her beloved dog had just tried to take her arm off. But it was clear she was going to need stitches. She pressed the tissues into her hand and squeezed them tight to stem the flow of blood as she kept a fixed stare on Velcro. The dog's soft whimpers broke my heart, and I draped an arm over Dianne's shoulders and gently squeezed.

"A lot of times when dogs are in stress, they involuntarily lash out," I said. "Trust me, she didn't mean to do it."

Dianne merely nodded as she continued to monitor the dog's movements.

"Is she going to be okay?"

"Josie is the best," I said. "And she will move heaven and earth to do everything she can."

"You didn't answer my question," Dianne whispered.

I gave her shoulder another soft squeeze.

"I'm not going to lie to you, Dianne. She's in pretty bad shape. But Josie will be working on her in ten minutes. That increases her chances a lot."

"Okay," she said, exhaling loudly.

"I can't believe I dropped the lead," I said as a wave of guilt washed over me.

"If you hadn't, I'd been the one going into surgery," she said. "Or worse."

I nodded and knelt down next to the dog, well out of reach of her mouth. I gently placed a hand on the dog's ribs, and Velcro reacted with a snap of her jowls and another round of whimpers. I pulled my hand back and stood up.

"The car hit her in the side," I said.

"And?"

"She's probably dealing with some internal bleeding," I said. "But if we're lucky, she didn't break her legs or hip."

I spotted the van roaring over the crest of the hill and Josie came to a screeching stop next to us. She immediately hopped out and headed for the back. She trotted toward us carrying a muzzle and a canvas sling with handles we used as a stretcher. Josie glanced around then knelt down next to the dog.

"She bit you, huh?" Josie said, reaching for the dog's head.

"Yes, she did," Dianne said, grasping her bloody hand.

"Don't take it personally," Josie said, then focused on Velcro. "Easy, Velcro," she whispered in a soothing tone. "Easy does it. I'm just going to slip this on."

I watched in awe as she effortlessly slid the muzzle on and secured it while avoiding the dog's attempts to take a chunk out of her hand.

"Okay," Josie said, from her knees. "Suzy, spread the stretcher next to her as close as you can. That's it, right up against her back. Dianne, I need you to come around to the other side. Kneel down, and when Suzy and I lift her, all you need to do is slide your hands under her and gently

145

ease her down onto the stretcher. I'll hold her head, Suzy. You'll need to get both hands under her back legs and lift. Easy, but as quickly as possible."

"Got it," I said, taking my position.

"You ready, Dianne?" Josie said.

"I am," Dianne said through tear-stained eyes.

"Okay, as soon as we get her onto the stretcher, we're going to walk her to the back of the van and slide her in. Then both of you will sit on either side of her on the drive. Keep her as still and quiet as you can without touching her if you can help it. Understand?"

Dianne and I both nodded. We followed Josie's instructions and soon the dog was in the back of the van. We climbed in and Josie hopped into the driver seat and made the short drive. She pulled into the parking lot no more than three minutes later and came to a stop directly in front of the steps that led into the registration area. Sammy and Jill, both dressed in sweats and running shoes, were already waiting on the front porch. Like an army general commanding her troops, Josie climbed out and began giving instructions as soon as she began walking to the back of the van.

146

"Sammy, give me a hand getting her in," Josie said. "Jill, I need you to make sure we're prepped for surgery. And I'm going to need X-rays."

"Got it," Jill said, then trotted inside.

Dianne and I watched Josie and Sammy carefully make their way up the steps. Then we climbed out of the van and entered the Inn.

"Have a seat."

"I'd like to be in there," Dianne said, staring at the door that led to the back of the Inn.

"No, you wouldn't," I said, shaking my head. "And we should get you to the emergency room to get that hand looked at."

"I'm not going anywhere," she said, sitting down.

"Sure, I understand," I said, then removed a towel and some gauze from the cabinet behind the registration desk. I ran the towel under hot water then sat down next to Dianne who continued to stare off into space. "Let's take a look at that hand."

"What?" she said, as if remembering I was in the room with her. "Oh, okay."

She held her hand out, and I removed the bloody tissues and held her arm by the wrist as I examined the wound.

"Geez, that's nasty," I said, frowning. "I think you might be typing with one hand for the next few weeks."

"That's the least of my concerns."

"Yeah," I whispered.

I wiped the blood away, noticed it was still seeping then wrapped the gauze around her hand tight and fastened it with tape.

"That'll hold it for now," I said, inspecting my work. "But try to keep your hand up if you can. That will help stop the bleeding."

She nodded and raised her hand as if about to ask a question.

"Josie will sew you up as soon as she finishes with Velcro."

Dianne nodded again then wailed loudly. Her cries soon transitioned into an extended round of muffled sobs, and I watched her, basically helpless to say or do anything to ease her suffering. Sometimes, you simply have to stand by in silence and let people try to cope with their grief.

We sat quietly for the next several minutes before Josie burst through the doors.

"Okay, here's the update," she said. "I've got her on an IV and gave her something for the pain. She cracked a couple of ribs, but her legs are fine. But her hip is dislocated. I'm going to put it back in place before I do surgery."

"Surgery?" Dianne said through wide-eyes.

"I'm afraid she's bleeding internally," Josie said. "I think the muscles have been torn away from her ribcage. I'm going to have to open her up."

Dianne began another extended round of wailing, and I placed a hand on her shoulder. I looked up at Josie.

"Is she going to be okay?" I whispered.

"We'll know soon," she said. "Look, why don't you two head up to the house? I'll be up as soon as I have more news."

Then she turned and disappeared through the doors.

"C'mon," I said, patting Dianne on the back. "Let's go have some coffee. You'll be more comfortable up there."

Dianne nodded and slowly got to her feet. Rather than take her out the back door and run the risk of her seeing what Josie was doing to Velcro, I led her out the front door and up the path to the house. We entered through the kitchen and all four house dogs greeted us. They soon sensed something was wrong and settled down immediately. Captain gently nudged Dianne's leg with his nose and wagged his tail like a metronome. Dianne couldn't help but chuckle softly, and she stroked the dog's head. I put on a pot of coffee then led her into the living room where Paulie and my mom were stretched out watching a movie. Queen, my mother's King Charles, was perched on her stomach keeping a watchful eye on the action. They both sat up when we entered and couldn't miss the look on our faces.

"What's the matter?" my mother said.

I gave her the short version as I petted Queen, and they listened closely and shared confused glances.

"What happened to your hand?" Paulie said.

"Velcro bit me," Dianne said.

They both nodded and my mom patted Dianne's knee affectionately.

"Try not to worry too much, dear," my mother said. "Josie is going to do everything she can."

"And more," Paulie said.

"How's Max doing?" I said, glancing down the hall.

"She's been an angel," my mother said. "She went down around eight, and we haven't heard a peep out of her since."

"I'm gonna go take a look," I said, then headed to my bedroom. I watched her, sound asleep in her crib and gave her a long, loving stare. Then I went back to the living room and sat down.

150

"Did you get a good look at the car?" Paulie said.

"No, it all happened so fast," Dianne said. "And then Velcro knocked me on my butt."

"How about you, Suzy?" he said.

"It was a black SUV," I said. "At least it looked black. It had its lights off."

"A black SUV?" Dianne said softly.

"Yes," I said, studying her face. "Why?"

"Selma rented a black SUV for the drive down," Dianne said.

"Huh," I grunted, already deep in thought. "Who's been driving it since she was killed?"

"It could be anyone," she said with a shrug. "Or all of them."

"But who took the keys?" I said.

"I have no idea," Dianne said, staring up at the ceiling.

"I almost forgot," I said, getting to my feet. "I need to call the Chief."

"Are you going to invite him over here?" my mother said.

"Now that I think about it, it's probably better if we meet him down at the Inn," I said. "I'd rather not do anything to wake Max up."

"Good call, darling," my mother said. "You two go ahead. We'll be fine here. But keep us posted."

"Thanks, Mom."

"Oh, one more thing," my mother said.

"What's that?"

"Please don't do anything stupid."

I made a face at her then gave her and Paulie a hug. We headed back down to the Inn, and I led Dianne to my office. I sat down behind my desk and made the call. As I waited, I spotted her craning her neck as if trying to hear what was going on in the surgery suite.

"We'll know soon enough," I said softly.

"Can't we poke our head in?"

"No," I said. "Just let Josie work her magic. She'll update us as soon as she knows anything."

Dianne nodded and slumped further down in the couch.

"Suzy? Why the hell are you calling me this late?"

"Sorry, Chief. But I need to see you. And bring Detective Williams and Agent Tompkins with you."

"Geez," the Chief whispered. "Who's dead?"

"Thankfully, nobody," I said. "But Dianne and I just had a very close call. And Josie is currently doing surgery on her dog."

152

"Somebody tried to kill her dog?" he said, annoyed.

"I'll tell you all about it when you get here," I said. "We're in my office at the Inn."

"Okay, I'll see you soon," he said, then ended the call.

"They're on their way?" Dianne said, snapping out of her stupor.

"They are," I said.

"What do you think is going on?" she said.

"I'm not sure," I said. "But the good news is that we finally know who the intended victim was."

"Somebody is trying to kill me, and you consider that good news?" she said, raising an eyebrow at me.

"Yeah, I suppose that didn't come out right," I said through a sheepish grin. "But now that we know you're the one on their radar, that should help narrow things down."

"If I were writing this, do you know what I'd be calling tonight's events?"

I gave it some thought then nodded.

"A mid-story reveal?"

"You are good," she said with a nod.

"Well, let's hope things turn out like your books do," I said, taking a sip of my coffee that was getting cold.

"How's that?"

153

"The good guys survive and prosper while the bad guys get it in the neck," I said.

"It's probably easier to write it than make it happen in real life," Dianne said.

I flashed back to the sight of Dianne sprawled out on the pavement and the dog suffering, writhing in pain, then focused on Dianne.

"Oh, don't worry. It's gonna happen."

Chapter 15

Chief Abrams was the first to arrive, followed soon after by Agent Tompkins and Detective Williams. The FBI agent went straight to his aunt and gave her a long hug. Dianne began another crying jag that lasted for several minutes. I tossed the agent a box of tissues and watched as he did his best to comfort her. As bad as she was, I knew I'd be in even worse shape if something similar had happened to Chloe or any of our other dogs.

We waited until Dianne composed herself then the Chief removed his notebook and flipped to a fresh page.

"Okay," he said, focusing on me. "Start at the beginning."

I did.

When I finished telling the story I sat back and waited for what I was sure would be several questions.

"The car was running without lights?" the Chief said.

"Yeah," I said softly. "It came over the crest of the hill and was on top of us before we knew it."

"And you're sure it was a black SUV?" Detective Williams said.

"Positive," I said.

"The same one the Blankenship woman rented?" the detective continued.

"I don't know," I said. "I didn't even know she had rented one."

The detective turned to Dianne. She returned his stare and shrugged.

"I didn't get a good look at the car," she said. "I was on the ground."

"What was in the middle of the road that caused you to stop in the first place?" the Chief said.

"A bag of trash," Dianne said. "Someone must have tossed it out of their car."

"Or put it there on purpose," I said, my neurons surging.

"Continue," the Chief said.

"If there was a bag like that in the middle of the street, most people would stop and remove it, right?"

"Maybe," the Chief said with a frown. "But for now, let's assume you're right."

"But how could anybody know it would be you who'd find it?" Detective Williams said.

"Somebody who was following us," I said. "From the hotel."

Detective Williams stood up and the Chief looked up at him.

"Where are you going?"

"To see if the bag is still there," the detective said. "And then I'm going to swing by the hotel and roust some people."

"We'll be here," the Chief said.

We watched the state cop depart. The Chief focused on Dianne who was sitting quietly staring off into space. She looked exhausted and another wave of sympathy washed over me.

"Dianne?" the Chief said.

"Yes."

"Do you have any idea who might want to kill you?" he said.

"No," she whispered.

"You fired Claudia yesterday," Agent Tompkins said.

"I did," she said. "But Claudia would never do anything like that. She's…unstable at times. But she's not a killer."

"Perhaps," the Chief said. "What do you think her life is going to be like now that she's no longer working for you?"

Dianne gave it some thought and, for a moment, I thought she was going to start crying again.

"Well, she still represents Joshua," she said eventually. "But I suppose she's going to have some difficulties. I'm the major source of her income."

"Is Joshua the only other author she represents?" the Chief said.

"Yes," Dianne said. "She's had trouble attracting other writers. Most people can't handle her…idiosyncrasies."

"How much do you know about her background?" the Chief said.

"I know everything she's willing to share," she said. "But she doesn't like to talk about her past, and I'm not one to push too hard. I do know that she was in and out of mental hospitals for a few years when she was younger."

"While she was working for you?" the Chief said.

"I don't think so," she said, then frowned.

"What is it?" Agent Tompkins said.

"A few years ago, she disappeared for a few months," Dianne said. "When she surfaced, she told me she'd been on vacation somewhere in Asia."

"Did that seem strange to you?" the Chief said. "You know, that she would just disappear like that?"

158

"Not really," Dianne said. "We'd both been working very hard and needed a break. I took some time off myself."

"Could she have been in the hospital or maybe some sort of clinic?" the Chief said.

Dianne gave it some thought then shrugged.

"I suppose it's possible," she whispered.

"We can certainly find out," Agent Tompkins said.

"What about Wilbur and Imelda?" I said.

"What about them?" Dianne said.

"Would your decision to leave Blankenship make them angry enough to want to kill you?" I said.

"No, I don't," she said. "I mean, why would they care? It was Selma's company. They just worked there." Then she chuckled softly. "As Selma loved to remind them every chance she got."

"How was the atmosphere around the office lately?" I said.

"What do you mean?" Dianne said.

"I'm just wondering if the office dynamics changed after Imelda dumped Selma for Wilbur," I said.

"How the heck did you know about that?" Dianne said.

"It came up while we were talking earlier," Agent Tompkins said.

"I asked you not to tell anyone about that," Dianne said, glancing over at her nephew. "It's nobody's business."

"I didn't tell her," he said. "She figured it out by herself."

Dianne stared at me and I merely shrugged.

"But to answer your question," she continued. "I could guess but I have no idea what the dynamics were. I rarely visited and Selma hated talking about it."

I remained silent, deep in thought. My mind kept circling back to Claudia as the most likely suspect, but something nagged at me. Eventually, it coalesced and I leaned forward.

"Did Claudia know you and Selma had switched rooms?"

Dianne gave it some thought then shook her head.

"I don't think so. I know I didn't mention it. I mean, why would I? It was just something we did to keep Velcro from barking at all the boats."

At the mention of the dog's name, Dianne teared up again and sobbed. Again, her nephew did his best to comfort her.

160

"How likely is it that someone could smother the wrong person?" I said, glancing back and forth at both cops.

"I've been wondering that myself," the Chief said.

"It's possible," Agent Tompkins said. "If it was done in the dark and the victim wasn't able to speak. It's a bit of a longshot, but I've certainly seen stranger things."

The office door opened and Detective Williams appeared in the doorway holding a plastic bag.

"Is that it?" Chief Abrams said.

"Yeah," the detective said. "I thought we'd get a jump on things. I'm heading to the hotel to do some interviews while you two go through this."

"Nice try, Detective," the Chief said with a small laugh. "You just don't want to dig through a bag of garbage."

"No, I can't say that I do," Detective Williams said. "But it will save us some time."

The Chief and Agent Tompkins looked at each other then shrugged.

"Okay, but you owe me," the Chief said to the detective as he got to his feet. "You want to do it in here?"

"Digging through a bag of garbage in my office? Not gonna happen," I said. "Use the registration area. There's a bunch of plastic gloves in the supply closet behind the desk."

"Got it," the Chief said, heading for the door.

"Are you going to be okay here?" Agent Tompkins said to his aunt.

"I'll be fine," she said.

"Have fun," I deadpanned.

"Yeah, I'm sure we're going to have a ball," the Chief said.

After they left, Dianne stretched out on the couch, and I put my feet up on my desk. Baffled by what had happened, as well as the possible motives behind it, I rocked back and forth in my chair and dozed off. I woke with a start and a leg cramp when Josie entered and sat down across from me. Both Dianne and I sat up and leaned forward with an expectant stare.

"She's going to be fine," Josie said, motioning for her to sit up. "Now, let's take a look at that hand."

"Oh, my goodness," Dianne said, jumping off the couch to give her a warm embrace. "Thank you, Josie. Thank you so much."

"Don't mention it," Josie said, flinching from the hug. "That's quite a grip you got there."

162

"I'm sorry," Dianne said, sitting down on the edge of the couch. "So, she's going to make a full recovery?"

"Eventually, yes," Josie said, unwrapping the bandage on Dianne's hand. "But she's going to need some time to get back on her feet."

"You were able to get the hip put back in place?" I said.

"We were," she said as she examined the wound. "Nasty. She got you good. When I put the joint back in place, it would have hurt like hell. Fortunately, she was out at the time. She'll be sore for several days, and I put a harness on her back leg to hold it in place. I'll be right back."

Josie left the office and soon returned with her bag and a wet towel. She wiped the hand clean, sterilized the wound, then injected a couple of spots with a numbing agent.

"Let's just give that a minute," she said, arching her back in a long stretch. "When Velcro's able to handle being on her feet, we'll get her started on the underwater treadmill."

"What?" Dianne said, resting her hand on the edge of the couch.

"We put in a hydrotherapy unit a few months ago," I said. "It's a low impact system. Very little resistance. The only problem is trying to keep the dogs out of it."

"Yeah, they love it," Josie said with a laugh. "I found Captain and Chloe using it the other day. The little buggers figured out how to turn the thing on. I still don't know how they managed to do that."

"What about the internal bleeding?" I said.

"One of her ribs nicked her stomach lining," Josie said. "I sewed it up and that seemed to do the trick. But I had to remove a small portion of the rib."

"What?" Dianne said.

"Don't worry, she'll never miss it," Josie said. "She's a lucky girl."

"Can I go see her?" Dianne said.

"Sure. Just as soon as we finish up here," Josie said as she began stitching the wound. "Sammy and Jill are getting her settled into a condo. But she's still out and will be for a few hours."

"Is it okay if I stay with her?" she said.

"I'd be surprised if you didn't," Josie said without looking up from her work.

A few minutes later, Josie examined her work, then nodded and applied a fresh bandage.

164

"There you go," she said, putting her instruments away.

"How many stitches?" Dianne said.

"Only seven."

"You do good work," she said as she took a quick look at her hand.

"Thanks," Josie said, taking a seat across from me. "I've been thinking about taking up needlepoint."

"What's stopping you?" Dianne said.

"I can't find anybody willing to sit still that long," Josie deadpanned.

Dianne laughed and shook her head.

"Can I go now?"

"My work is done," Josie said through a yawn.

Dianne literally trotted out of the office and Josie took her place on the couch. She stretched out and closed her eyes.

"Thank you," I said. "Well done."

"All in a day's work," she said, shrugging it off. "But that is one lucky dog. A foot to either side and we probably wouldn't be having this conversation."

"Still, great job," I said, beaming at her.

"You can reward me with a bite-sized."

I found a half-eaten bag in my desk drawer and tossed it to her. She sat up, tore the wrapper and popped one into her mouth.

"I have a question," she said through a mouthful of chocolate.

"What's on your mind?"

"I'm just wondering. I'm so tired, I might have started hallucinating."

"What?"

"Did I just see Agent Tompkins and the Chief digging through a bag of garbage in registration?"

"You did."

"Okay," she said, nodding through another yawn. "Should I ask why?"

"It's potential evidence."

"If you say so. Just one more question before I go to sleep."

"What's that?"

"They are going to clean up their mess, right?"

"They are."

"Good. Goodnight."

"Aren't you going up to the house?"

"No, I'm going to take a nap down here then check on Velcro. Turn the light off on your way out, please."

166

"Will do. Thanks again."

"Don't mention it," she managed to mumble.

I got up and headed for the door. I grabbed a blanket from the closet and draped it over her. Then I switched off the light and headed for registration, once again amazed by the skills and modesty my best friend and partner possessed and displayed on a daily basis.

Chapter 16

I stood in the doorway leading to the registration area and chuckled at the sight. Chief Abrams, wearing plastic gloves was sitting on the floor, legs splayed and digging through the garbage bag. Agent Tompkins was kneeling next to him and inspecting various items the Chief tossed his way. Eventually, I entered and sat down in a nearby chair.

"You guys missed your calling," I deadpanned.

"Funny," the Chief said without looking up. "You want to give us a hand?"

"Not a chance," I said. "I don't do garbage at three in the morning."

"Your loss," the Chief said as he removed a couple of empty soda cans. Then he turned the bag upside down and shook it gently. Satisfied it was empty, he tossed the bag to one side and glanced around at the collection. "Well, at least it didn't have too many sticky surprises."

"Yeah. But still, it's been a long time since I've done anything this disgusting," Agent Tompkins said as he got

168

off his knees and sat with his back against a couch. "You see anything interesting?"

"Not yet," the Chief said as he continued to examine various objects.

I leaned forward and propped a hand under my chin as I scanned the mess on the floor.

"How about you?" Agent Tompkins said.

"No," I said, sitting back and draping a leg over my knee. Then a thought bubbled to the surface and I leaned forward again. "You know what it looks like?"

"Downtown after the 4th of July?" the Chief said.

"Besides that," I said with a laugh. "I could be wrong, but I think that's a collection of car trash. Somebody cleaned their car and put it in that bag."

"Huh?" the Chief grunted.

All three of us looked around at the collection of empty Styrofoam cups, old newspapers, candy wrappers, several beer cans and other remnants of items found at any convenience store.

"I think you might be right," Chief Abrams said.

"I'm not sure it gets us any closer," Agent Tompkins said.

"Probably not," I said. "But we know for a fact the garbage didn't come from that SUV."

Both cops stared at me.

"Do you have any idea what she's talking about?" Agent Tompkins said to the Chief.

"Not a clue," he said. "But I'm sure she's going to explain it."

"Look around," I said. "That's road-trip garbage. Does that look like the car trash produced by Selma and her group? Slim Jim wrappers and a five-dollar, six-pack of beer?"

"No, it doesn't," Agent Tompkins said. "You're saying somebody brought the bag of garbage with them when they decided to run Aunt Dianne over?"

"Yeah, I think I am," I said, frowning.

"Who the heck would do that?" the Chief said.

"A crazy person with a half-baked idea?" I said with a shrug. "Somebody trying to come up with a diversion that would get us to stop and take a look at the bag?"

I realized how strange it sounded as soon as I said it out loud. A frown formed on both their faces as I talked, and when I stopped, I added my look of confusion to the mix.

"If we assume it was a nutjob who tried to run her over," Agent Tompkins said.

"Like Claudia," the Chief interjected.

170

"Exactly," Agent Tompkins said. "But if we make the assumption all this trash didn't come from the SUV, where did it come from?"

"Maybe she went dumpster-diving," the Chief said.

"I wouldn't put it past her," Agent Tompkins said.

"No, I don't think so," I said, trying to force my jumbled thoughts to coalesce.

"Why not?" the Chief said.

"It would make the attempt on Dianne's life premeditated," I said.

"Somebody put a bag of garbage in the road then waited for her to walk out into the middle of the street," Agent Tompkins said. "How much more premeditated could it be?"

"No, I get that," I said, frowning. "But I think the plan was developed on the spot without a lot of prior planning. I think whoever it was watched us leave the hotel, followed us for a while, then hatched their plan on the spot. It was premeditated, but only in the moment. If that makes any sense."

"I don't know, Suzy," the Chief said. "I think you're jumping to a whole bunch of conclusions."

"If I didn't, I'd never get any exercise."

They both laughed and I again sat back and draped a leg over my knee. I gently rubbed my forehead before taking another look around at the pile of trash on the floor. Then I leaned forward again when something caught my eye.

"What's that piece of glass buried in all those candy wrappers?" I said.

"Oh, that's an empty whiskey bottle," Agent Tompkins said.

My neurons surged and I almost came out of my chair.

"It's not a Hiram Walker bottle by any chance, is it?" I whispered.

Agent Tompkins reached for the bottle and carefully held it up in the air with two fingers. Then he stared at me.

"How the hell did you know that?"

"Lucky guess," I said, my mind racing.

"Suzy?" the Chief said. "How did you know that?"

I spent a few minutes telling the story of the odd stranger who'd been at Dianne's presentation and the restaurant. I recounted my perfunctory conversation with the man at the bar then sat back in my chair, deep in thought.

"You don't know who he is?" the Chief said.

"Only that his first name is Hiram," I said.

"What possible reason could he have for trying to kill Aunt Dianne?"

"I have no idea," I said. And I didn't. A flood of questions surged through me, and I chewed softly on my bottom lip. "If somebody were following us, it wouldn't take them long to stage the scene in the street, right?"

"No," the Chief said. "And there are enough side streets off of Church to stay out of sight. They could have dropped the bag then taken up their position at the top of the hill. And given the time of night, there's a good chance no other cars would have come by."

"So, I'm not completely crazy," I said.

"Rhetorical, right?" the Chief said with a grin. Then his phone buzzed and he answered it on the second ring. "Hey, Detective Williams. Hang on, I'm putting you on speaker."

"Who's there?" Detective Williams said.

"I'm here with Suzy and Agent Tompkins," the Chief said. "Did you get a chance to talk to them?"

"I did," the detective said. "It looks like their alibis might hold up. After they got back from the restaurant tonight, they all had a nightcap in the hotel bar. Then they all headed up to their rooms just before one."

"That was right around the time it happened," I said, then a question floated to the surface. "After Selma got killed, who took possession of the car keys?"

"Her assistant Imelda."

"Does she still have them?" the Chief said.

"No, she doesn't," Detective Williams said.

"Interesting. Did they drive to the restaurant tonight?" I said.

"No, they walked."

"Where did she have the keys?" Agent Tompkins said.

"She left them under the floor mat on the driver side," Detective Williams said.

"Why on earth would she do that?" the Chief said.

"I was wondering that myself," he said. "She did it so anybody could take the car whenever they needed. And since Clay Bay is such a small town, she didn't think anybody would mess with it."

"That sounds pretty thin," Agent Tompkins said. "Do you believe her?"

"Maybe," the detective said. "You'd think that somebody who lived in New York would know better."

"Yeah," the Chief said. "One would think."

"Imelda said no one has driven the car since they arrived," Detective Williams said. "I've got my guys out looking for it. So far, no sign of it."

"It'll turn up," the Chief said. "And probably abandoned."

"Yeah, whoever it was wouldn't be dumb enough to keep driving it around," the detective said. "Have you guys found anything?"

"Maybe," Agent Tompkins said. "You mind sending one of your techs over here? We've got a whiskey bottle I'd like to check for prints."

"A whiskey bottle," Detective Williams said. "Sure, I'll send somebody over as soon as I get off the phone. Should I swing by as well?"

The Chief and Agent Tompkins looked at each other and they both nodded.

"Yeah, that's probably a good idea," Agent Tompkins said. "We might have a working theory coming together you need to hear."

"I'm on my way," he said, then ended the call.

"Okay," Agent Tompkins said, getting to his feet. "You mind if we talk in your office?"

"No, that's fine. As long as Josie is up," I said, watching the FBI agent as he started to head off. "Hey, hang on."

"What?" he said, coming to a stop.

"Aren't you forgetting something?" I said, pointing at the pile of trash.

"Oh, right," he said, then knelt down next to the Chief. Then he glanced up at me. "Aren't you going to give us a hand?"

"No," I said with a grin. "You guys can handle it. I'm going to head up to the house to check on Max and the dogs. I'll be back in ten. Have fun."

I headed out the front door and up the path to the house with my mind racing down a long set of tracks with no clear destination in sight.

Chapter 17

I slowly opened the kitchen door and made my way inside, doing my best not to disturb the dogs. But Chloe, wide awake and bouncing at my feet, appeared as soon as I stepped inside. I knelt down to rub her head and ears.

"Hey, Little Girl. What are you doing up?" I said as she nuzzled my neck.

"She's been keeping me company."

I looked up at Chef Claire as she refilled her wine glass.

"You want a glass?"

"No, I better not," I said. "Why aren't you in bed?"

"I'm still too keyed up," she said, nodding for me to follow her out onto the front verandah.

The other three house dogs were sprawled out but leapt to their feet when they spotted me. After saying hello to all of them, I sat down at the table across from her.

"Busy night, huh?" I said.

"Our biggest ever," she said. "We did over six hundred dinners tonight."

"Six hundred?" I said, baffled. "How is that even possible?"

"We still had a ton of people waiting after our last seating. So, I decided to add another. We didn't get out of the kitchen until almost one, and we ran out of almost everything. I'm exhausted, but the adrenaline is still kicking around."

"A couple of glasses of wine will fix that," I said. "Have you heard any noises coming from Max's room?"

"Not a peep. Your mom said she's been sound asleep since she put her down."

"I'm going to check on her. I'll be right back."

I looked in on Max who was sound asleep. As I always did, I watched her closely until I was sure her breathing pattern was normal then headed back to the verandah. I stretched out in a lounge chair and spent the next few minutes petting the dogs. Then Chloe hopped up on the lounger and stretched out at my feet. I again waved off Chef Claire's offer of wine.

"A little past your bedtime, isn't it?" Chef Claire said.

"It's been a night."

I recounted the evening's events and she listened closely. When I finished, she shook her head in disbelief and refilled her glass.

"So, whoever killed the publisher got the wrong person?" Chef Claire said.

"Yeah, that's the way it looks."

"The poor woman."

"Which one?" I said.

"Well, both of them," she said. "But I was referring to the publisher. One minute you're sleeping peacefully, the next you wake up with a pillow over your face. Josie's sure the dog is going to be okay?"

"She is," I said, nodding. "The dog saved Dianne's life." I sat up on the lounger causing Chloe to give me the stink eye. I found her look funny and I laughed as I reached down to rub her head. "I'm sorry to interrupt your beauty sleep, your majesty. But duty calls."

"How's Agent Tompkins doing? I haven't had a chance to say hi to him."

"He's obviously worried about his aunt, but other than that, he's good. You want to tag along?"

"I'm dealing with a dozen layers of dirt and sweat, and I reek of kitchen. I'm going to take a long shower then hit the sack. Tomorrow is going to be a zoo, again."

"Got it," I said as I got to my feet. I gave her a long hug. "You're right. You do stink."

"Don't say I didn't warn you," she said, reaching down with both hands to pet Al and Dente who were hovering close. "I'll see you in the morning."

"It's already morning," I said, then waved and said goodbye to the dogs before heading down the path back to the Inn.

I arrived just as Detective Williams was pulling into the parking lot. I waited for him and we walked in together. Josie was rummaging through the registration desk and she glanced up at us.

"Have you seen my book?" she said.

"The new Connelly?" I said.

"Yeah. I can't find it anywhere."

"I think it's in my room. You want me to run up and get it?"

"No, don't worry about it. Hey, Detective Williams."

"Hi, Josie. How's the dog doing?"

"She's gonna make it. But it's going to take her a while. I'll see you guys later."

She headed for the condo area and we went to my office where Chief Abrams and Agent Tompkins were already waiting. We exchanged perfunctory greetings before getting to the business at hand.

"I just spoke with my tech," Detective Williams said. "He's on his way. What did you find in the garbage bag?"

"Remnants of road food," Agent Tompkins said. "Convenience store trash of someone who'd been driving for at least a day. Maybe longer."

"Unless he was a major snacker," I said.

"Well, if anybody would know..." the Chief deadpanned.

"Funny."

"Tell me about the whiskey bottle," Detective Williams said.

"It's a Hiram Walker bottle," Agent Tompkins said.

"Okay," the detective said, frowning. "Is that supposed to mean something to me?"

Agent Tompkins glanced over at me and motioned for me to explain.

"There was a strange guy in the bar at C's," I said. "We had a brief conversation but he told me his name was Hiram. And it sounded like his father was an alcoholic."

"And you somehow put those two things together?" the detective said, obviously not impressed by the news. "I think I'm missing something here."

"I know it's a bit of a stretch," I said. "But if the guy's old man was that big of a drinker, it's possible he named his kid after his favorite booze."

"And you think the guy followed in his father's footsteps?" Detective Williams said.

"It's possible," I said with a shrug.

"Geez, Suzy," the detective said. "I've learned the hard way not to question your theories too much, but this one is a bit…on the nose."

"You got anything better?" I said softly, too tired to get cranky with him.

"I do not," Detective Williams said. "But what possible motive could he have for trying to kill Dianne?"

"I have no idea," I said with a shrug. "But the vacant stare in his eyes really stuck with me."

"And you think he was staking out the hotel and spotted the two of you taking a late-night walk?" Detective Williams said.

"That's the best explanation I can come up with," I said.

"Okay," he said, far from convinced. "Let's call it a working theory for now."

"You're being generous," I said with a chuckle.

"Did he pay his bar tab with a credit card?" Detective Williams said.

"No, he paid cash. He slid a couple of twenties under his glass then left."

"Did you get a chance to talk to Millie about him?" the Chief said.

"Not really," I said, shaking my head. "But she picked up on how strange he was."

"I'll touch base with her later," Chief Abrams said.

We heard a soft knock on the door, and Detective Williams got up to answer it. I recognized the tech standing in the doorway and gave him a small wave.

"The whiskey bottle is on the end table next to the garbage bag," Agent Tompkins said.

We sat in silence until Detective Williams returned. I was exhausted and had to force myself to keep from nodding off.

"Is my aunt out back with Velcro?" Agent Tompkins said.

"She is," I said.

"I'm going to go check on them," he said, getting to his feet. "I'll be back soon."

Detective Williams flipped through the pages in his notepad then gave up and slid it back into his pocket.

183

"I thought this case might get a bit easier as soon as we figured out who the intended victim was," the detective said. "I think I was wrong. Was there anything else about the guy that stood out?"

"Not really," I said. "It was a very short conversation. But it was pretty clear he's disturbed."

"That's putting it mildly. He killed one woman and did his best to kill another," the Chief said.

"If Suzy's theory is correct," Detective Williams said.

"No, whether he did it or not," I said. "It was pretty clear the guy has a lot of issues he's dealing with."

My neurons flared and I sat up in my chair.

"What's the matter?" the Chief said. "You've got that look."

"I'm not sure," I said, rubbing my forehead. "But something's nagging at me."

"It'll come to you," the Chief said. "At least, I sure hope it does. Because I've got nothing."

Detective Williams' phone buzzed and he answered on the first ring.

"Williams. Hey, Jimmy. What's up?" The detective listened closely and nodded several times as he scribbled notes. "Okay, hang tight. We're on our way." He slid his phone into his pocket and glanced back and forth at us. "My guys found the car."

"Where is it?" the Chief said.

"Bailey Road near the state park," Detective Williams said. "I'll go grab Agent Tompkins and meet you guys out front."

We headed outside and the Chief and I climbed into my car. I started the engine and waited until I saw the two other cops climb into Detective Williams vehicle, then followed them out of the parking lot.

"The state park is pretty remote," Chief Abrams said. "A long walk home."

"The closest motel is the Keeler's place," I said, inserting a CD into the player. "It's gotta be four or five miles from there, right?"

"At least," the Chief said, nodding as the music started. "Miles Davis. Good call."

"Yeah, Nefertiti," I said. "It's incredible."

We rode in silence and let the music wash over us. Ten minutes later, I made a right and followed Detective Williams' car. Thick stands of pines surrounded us on both sides and we soon spotted a clearing where the SUV and a state police car were parked on the side of the road. The Chief and I climbed out and made the short walk.

"I haven't been out here in ages," I said, glancing around. "This used to be my favorite place to going parking with my boyfriend."

"Really?" the Chief said, laughing. "Do tell."

"Not a chance," I said, gently punching him on the shoulder. I recognized the uniformed state cop and waved as we approached. "Hi, Jimmy."

"Hey, Suzy," the cop said. "What brings you out here?"

"That," I said, pointing at the SUV.

"Thanks for the call, Jimmy," Detective Williams said. "What have we got?"

"Not a lot," he said. "I took a chance and drove down here just in case, you know?"

"Yeah. I'm glad you did," Detective Williams said. "Did you find anything?"

"The keys are in the ignition," Jimmy said, turning on a flashlight and shining it on the driver side door. "But it looks like it's been wiped clean."

"It does," Detective Williams said. "But let's see if we can pull some prints."

"Will do," Jimmy said, heading to his car.

Detective Williams put his hands on his hips and glanced around through the darkness.

"Odd place to leave it," he said.

"He didn't want anybody to find it for a while," the Chief said.

"Still, it's a long walk to anywhere from here," Detective Williams said.

"Unless he had somebody waiting to pick him up," the Chief said.

"That makes the most sense," Detective Williams said, nodding.

I glanced around the immediate area then flinched when I stepped on something that snapped loudly.

"Hey, Chief, shine your flashlight on my foot," I said.

"Did you cut yourself?" the Chief said, staring down at the broken glass.

"No," I said. "But is that what I think it is?"

The Chief knelt down and picked up a large piece of glass with part of the label still attached to it.

"Hiram Walker," he said, handing it to Detective Williams.

"It's wet," Agent Tompkins said. "He must have dropped it on his way out."

"Or he broke it in a fit of rage," I said.

"Some sort of weird tribute to his old man?" Agent Tompkins said, shining his flashlight over the ground. "I gotta meet this guy."

"Take some backup with you when you do," the Chief said, jotting down a note in his pad. "I'll swing by the liquor stores later to see if anybody remembers a guy buying a bottle of Hiram Walker."

"And we'll need to touch base with all the motels in the area," Detective Williams said.

"Yeah, I don't think this guy is the hotel type," Agent Tompkins said.

"Hang on," I said. Then I held out my hand. "Let me borrow your flashlight, Chief."

"Okay."

"Follow me," I said, heading toward the pines.

"Where are we going?" Agent Tompkins said.

"Down," I said. "He came by boat."

I scanned the area for the entry point. I finally located it and they followed me as I made my down a winding, overgrown path.

"What the heck is this?" Agent Tompkins said.

"It leads down to the water," I said, hunching down under various pine boughs growing across the path. "Not a lot of people know about it. At least, they didn't use to."

188

"Don't tell me," the Chief said, laughing. "You and your boyfriend used to spread a blanket out on top of the pine needles."

"Only once," I said, swatting at a bug about to take a chunk out of my forearm. "The mosquitos were brutal."

I stopped when I spotted a candy wrapper on the path. It was the same brand we'd found several of in the trash bag.

"This guy needs to lift his game. He has terrible taste in candy," I said, watching Detective Williams kneel down and slide the wrapper into an evidence bag.

"That's the least of his problems," the Chief said.

We resumed our journey and I came to a stop on a small crest of granite that overlooked the River. In the moonlight, the water was calm and inviting, and I harkened back to the late-night swims my boyfriend and I had enjoyed during high school.

"It looks like quite a climb down," Detective Williams said.

"It is," I said. "But definitely manageable. If you know where you're going."

"Is there a dock down there?" the Chief said.

"No," I said, shining the beam at a spot about thirty feet below us. "But there's a flat patch of rock you can easily pull your boat onto."

"The guy comes in by boat with a bag of trash? And then walks five miles into town carrying it?" Detective Williams said. "C'mon, Suzy. You're better than that."

"That is a problem, isn't it?" I said with a deep frown.

"Even if this guy is as big of a nutjob as you think he is, yeah, it's a total stretch," Detective Williams said.

"Hang on," Agent Tompkins said. "You said he was at the bar earlier in the day. Are there trash receptacles at the town dock?"

"Sure," the Chief said. "A lot of people with summer places drop their trash off all the time when they come to town."

"Maybe he threw it away earlier in the day and went back for it tonight when he was looking to create the diversion," Agent Tompkins said.

"Geez, Agent Tompkins," Detective Williams said, shaking his head. "You're worse than her."

"Hey, watch it," I snapped, then gave Agent Tompkins' comment some thought. "Or he stashed the bag somewhere near the scene earlier in the day."

"Maybe," the Chief said. "But I still like the idea he had somebody helping him."

"Claudia?" I said, glancing around at all three cops.

"She definitely fits the description," Detective Williams said.

"Wingnut," the Chief said.

"Yeah," the detective said. "One nutjob helping out another."

"No," Agent Tompkins said, shaking his head. "I've known Claudia a long time. I can't believe she would do anything to hurt my aunt."

"Even though she just fired her?" Detective Williams said. "You said yourself it could ruin Claudia's life. What's left of it."

"I just don't see it," Agent Tompkins said.

But it was pretty clear from the look on his face he was definitely considering it a possibility. I glanced back out at the River and let my mind wander.

"Given all the trash in the bag, how long do you think he was in the car?" I said.

"Who knows?" the Chief said. "That garbage could have been in his car for weeks."

"I know," I said. "But assuming it built up while he was driving, how long of a drive do you think he made?"

191

"At least a full day," the Chief said. "Maybe longer."

"That means we're looking at a radius up to several hundred miles," Agent Tompkins said.

"Maybe even more," Detective Williams said. "From any direction."

"Which does nothing other than lead us in a circle," the Chief said. "We could end up chasing our tail for months."

"I hate when that happens," I said, then an idea floated to the surface. It certainly wasn't a good one, but it was the best I could come up with. "Hiram Walker is made in Canada."

"Not again," Detective Williams said. "You're back to the whiskey bottle?"

"You're starting to piss me off, Detective Williams," I said, glaring at him.

"Suzy, it's five o'clock in the morning, and I'm standing out here getting eaten alive by mosquitos," he said, his voice rising. "You'll have to excuse me if I don't find your latest theory fascinating."

"Just give me a minute," I said, swatting at a bug. "If we assume the guy drove in from Canada, he would have gone through Customs and Immigration."

"Of course," the Chief said, nodding.

"And they have cameras on all the cars crossing the border," I said.

"After 9/11, you can count on it," Agent Tompkins said.

"So, there might still be a record and a timestamp when he crossed," I said.

"I have no idea how long they keep those recordings," he said with a shrug. "But it's definitely worth following up on."

"And if I'm right he drove down from Canada, then by boat to Clay Bay, there's a good chance we know what island he's staying on."

"Wellesley," the Chief said, nodding. "Well done."

"I'm not following," Agent Tompkins said.

"Wellesley Island is one of the biggest islands around," the Chief said.

"And the bridge system that connects the U.S. and Canada runs right through it," I said.

"He drives to Wellesley and then comes here by boat," the Chief said. "It's certainly possible. People do it all the time."

"And if he knew about this place, there's a good chance he's spent some summers here," I said.

193

"We're going to need a whole lot more, Suzy," Detective Williams said.

"I know," I said, nodding. "Hang on."

"She has more," the detective said, shaking his head.

"Actually, I do." I looked at Agent Tompkins. "Didn't Dianne say that Claudia could have spent time in some sort of mental health facility a couple of years ago?"

"She did," he said.

"I wonder if she had company," I said softly.

"This guy Hiram?" Agent Tompkins said.

"Yeah," I said, nodding. "How hard would it be to find out?"

"You got his last name?"

"No," I said. "But how many nutjobs named Hiram can there be?"

"I'm sure we could find out," the FBI agent said. "But it wouldn't be quick. Especially if we have to subpoena the records. Places like that have a strict confidentiality policy. And if the facility was in Canada, I have no idea how long that would take."

"It's always something, right?" I said, deep in thought.

"Welcome to my world," Agent Tompkins said.

"Well, then I guess the only other thing to do is to ask her," I said.

"Claudia?" the Chief said.

"Yeah."

"I suppose I could bring her by the station for questioning," he said.

"No, let's not do that," I said. "Let's invite her to breakfast. I'm starving."

The Chief shined his flashlight on his watch then nodded.

"I could eat."

Chapter 18

I dropped the Chief off at his office then headed home. I checked in on the still sleeping Max before taking a long, hot shower. When I came out of the bathroom, toweling my hair, I found her wide awake and staring up at me. I tossed the towel in the hamper then gently lifted her out of the crib.

"Look who's finally awake," I cooed as I rocked her back and forth in my arms. "Ooh, somebody needs a change."

I set her down on the basinet and chattered as I changed her.

"Your mama had a long night. Crazy people everywhere you look. Yes, we've got quite the conundrum here. What do you think, Max?"

She kicked her legs and held her hands in the air. I lifted her into my arms and headed for the living room where my mother and Paulie were already up and sipping coffee.

"Good morning," my mother said. "I can't believe how long she slept."

"You wore her out, Mom," I said. "Are you hungry, Sweetie?"

Max gurgled. It was as close to a yes I could get out of her so I handed her to my mom then headed to the kitchen. A few minutes later, I returned with a bottle of milk and sat on the couch holding her and watching as she went to work.

"I must have been out like a log," Paulie said. "I didn't hear you come in last night."

"I was here briefly around three. But I just got back," I said, then launched into the events of last night.

My mother and Paulie listened closely. When I finished, I glanced down at Max who was already halfway through the bottle.

"I wonder who she gets that from," my mother said, laughing.

"Funny, Mom."

"This guy sounds dangerous," Paulie said.

"Yeah, I'm sure he is," I said. "But don't worry, I'm traveling with three cops."

"Still," Paulie said. "Why don't you let them handle it from here?"

"Rhetorical, right?" I said through a small smile.

"I forgot who I was talking to," he said, then took a sip of coffee.

"Darling, why don't you just leave it to them? You must be exhausted. I'll watch Max. Go to bed."

"I'll get a nap later," I said, then checked my watch. "I've got a breakfast meeting to get to."

I said my goodbyes then headed down to the Inn. I entered through the back and said good morning to all the dogs as I made my way to Velcro's condo. I peered inside and spotted Josie and Dianne sound asleep with their backs propped up against the wall. The Vizsla was stretched out on her bed and also asleep. I gently tapped the thick glass then entered. Both women stirred and slowly woke up.

"Good morning," I said.

"Hey," Josie said. "What time is it?"

"A little before seven," I said. "You guys been here all night?"

"We have," Dianne said, still groggy. She sat up and took a long, loving look at her dog then settled back against the wall. "She hasn't moved."

"Good," Josie said. "The less movement the better for the next few days."

"I need to run," I said. "Could you ask Sammy to handle the orders today?"

"Will do," she said. "Where are you off to?"

"I'm having breakfast with the cops," I said, then glanced at Dianne. "And Claudia."

"Claudia?" Dianne said. "Can I ask you why?"

"Basically, we're just following up on a hunch."

"Don't tell me you think she's involved in this," she said.

"To be honest, Dianne, I'm not sure what I think," I said. "Do you remember when we were talking about the time Claudia disappeared for a while a couple of years ago?"

"Her vacation," she said, nodding. "Sure."

"We're wondering if she spent that time in some sort of mental health facility."

"Like I said, I suppose it's possible."

"Would she have told you if she did?"

"Not a chance," Dianne said, shaking her head. "She'd be too embarrassed to admit something like that."

"Okay," I said, nodding. "I'll see you guys later. The panel discussion is at two, right?"

"It is."

"I'll see you there, if not before," I said, departing with a wave.

I made the short trip to the hotel and drove past the scene of the accident. I stopped without getting out and surveyed the shrubbery on the far side of the street. Deciding it would have been relatively easy to hide a bag of trash nearby, I put the car in drive and pulled into the hotel parking lot a minute later. I headed inside to the restaurant and spotted the three cops at a table.

"Good morning," the Chief said.

"Did you get a nap?" I said.

"I got about an hour in my office," he said.

"Hi, guys," I said to the other two. "Any sign of Claudia?"

"I just called her," Agent Tompkins said. "She's on her way."

"How do you want to handle it?" I said.

"Let's just get her talking," Agent Tompkins said. "A lot of times, once she gets rolling, she doesn't stop."

"Sounds good," I said, sitting back in my chair to make room for our server who was pouring coffee. "Thanks, Samantha."

"How's the baby, Suzy?" she said.

"Perfect," I said with a grin.

"Good answer," she said, then departed.

Moments later, Claudia appeared in the doorway. She looked around the dining room then spotted us and trudged our way. When she arrived at the table, she took one look at her chair then shook her head and walked away.

"Let's hope she orders something that doesn't require a knife," Detective Williams said.

"That was odd," Chief Abrams said. "Where the heck is she going?"

"Footstool," Agent Tompkins and I said in unison.

"What?" Detective Williams said.

"You'll see," Agent Tompkins said.

Claudia returned carrying a leather ottoman. She set it down, removed the chair, then slid the stool next to the table and knelt on it. Detective Williams and the Chief stared at her in disbelief. I sipped my coffee, hoping it would soon begin to work its magic.

"Much better," Claudia said, glancing around the table. "What did you want to talk about?"

As we had discussed earlier, Agent Tompkins took the lead.

"We thought you should know that someone tried to kill my aunt last night?" he said softly.

Claudia flinched and almost toppled off her perch. The Chief reached a hand out to steady her and Claudia took a long gulp of water. She brushed a strand of hair away from her face before focusing on Detective Williams.

201

"Is that why you woke me up last night?" Claudia said.

"It is," the detective said.

"Why didn't you tell me last night?"

It was a good question and I focused on the detective.

"It would have been premature," he said, deflecting.

"You were trying to see if I had an alibi, right?" she whispered.

"Yes," Detective Williams said. "I'm sorry for not being straight with you, Claudia, but I wasn't ready to go into the details."

Claudia shrugged it off and stared out through the picture windows that overlooked the River.

"Why would anybody want to kill Dianne?"

"We were hoping you might be able to help us out with that," Agent Tompkins said.

"Me? Why would I know anything about it?"

"Well, you two are so close," the FBI agent continued. "We were wondering if you might have heard or seen anything lately that could be considered suspicious."

"First, Selma. Now this," Claudia said, tearing up. "This is too much to deal with. I need to go back to bed. You'll have to excuse me."

"No, Claudia," Agent Tompkins said firmly. "I'm afraid you're going to have to talk with us. Hopefully, it won't take long."

Claudia looked back and forth at us with a wild-eyed stare, but she eventually nodded and knelt erect with a stone-faced expression. She took several deep breaths before speaking.

"Okay," was all she managed to get out.

"Have you recently seen anything out of the ordinary?" Agent Tompkins said.

"You mean, apart from Selma being smothered in her sleep?" she said without emotion.

"Yes, apart from that," Agent Tompkins said.

"Well, you just said somebody tried to kill Dianne," Claudia said with a shrug. "I didn't see it, but that seems out of the ordinary."

"Nothing gets past you," I said under my breath.

"What?"

"I'm just trying to decide what to eat," I said, my face flushed with embarrassment.

I caught the dirty look Agent Tompkins was giving me and buried my face behind my menu.

"But to answer your question," Claudia said. "It's been strange lately, but nothing out of the ordinary."

"Strange how?" Agent Tompkins said.

"I really need to get my nails done," she said, studying her hands.

"There's a salon here in the hotel," I said.

"Really?" she said, doing her best to focus on me. "That's wonderful news. I'll be right back."

She climbed off the ottoman and strolled out of the restaurant. We watched her disappear from sight.

"How many meds is she on?" Detective Williams said.

"According to my aunt, a lot."

"I think she might have double-dipped this morning," the Chief said. "She's out of it."

"She tends to over medicate when she's under stress," Agent Tompkins said.

"Why on earth did it take your aunt so long to fire her?" Detective Williams said. "That woman is freaking me out."

"The best explanation I have is a combination of loyalty and sympathy," Agent Tompkins said.

Claudia returned and trudged back to the table. She knelt back down on the ottoman and glanced at me.

"You were right," she said. "But they're closed at the moment."

204

"Good to know," I said, forcing a smile at her. "I think I'm going to go with the pancakes."

The rest of the group studied their menus until our server returned to take our orders. She worked her way around the table then came to Claudia.

"I'd like spaghetti and meatballs," she said, fixing a rheumy gaze on the waitress.

"I beg your pardon?" she said.

"Spaghetti and meatballs," Claudia repeated.

The waitress caught my eye and I nodded at her.

"Okay," she said softly. "Spaghetti and meatballs coming right up."

She left with a shake of her head and I made a mental note to over tip her.

"Interesting breakfast choice," Detective Williams said.

"Yes, I thought so, too," Claudia said. "What were we talking about?"

"Out of the ordinary things," Detective Williams said.

"Oh, that's right," she said. "No, I haven't seen anything like that."

"I'd love to hear your definition," the detective said.

"What?"

"Nothing," he said, then sipped coffee.

"So, you don't have any idea who might want to hurt Dianne?" Agent Tompkins said.

"No one I'm in regular contact with, no," Claudia said without making eye contact.

I frowned at her strange choice of words and turned to Agent Tompkins who was also doing his best to process the response.

"Now?" I whispered to him.

He gave it some thought then nodded. I looked at Claudia and spoke to her in a loud, clear voice.

"Oh, I almost forgot to tell you. Hiram said to say hello."

Claudia wheeled around on the footstool to look at me and lost her balance. She fell off the padded leather and landed with a loud thud that drew the attention of other diners. The Chief hopped out of his chair to help her up.

"I think she knows him," Agent Tompkins said. "Well done."

"Thanks," I said as I watched Claudia do her best to get comfortable on the hassock.

Claudia stared off into space and we waited it out. Eventually, she managed to focus on me.

"Hiram? That's an unusual name," she whispered.

"It is," I said. "Where did you two meet?"

206

"What makes you think I know anybody named Hiram?" Claudia said, her eyes again drifting off.

"Well, my first clue was when he told me to say hi to you," I said with a shrug.

"Yes, I can see how that might confuse you," she said.

"Claudia," Agent Tompkins said sharply. "That's enough."

She stared at the FBI agent as tears welled up then streamed down her cheeks.

"I met Hiram when I was…on vacation," she eventually managed to get out.

"Okay,' Agent Tompkins whispered. "Where were you *vacationing*?"

"Canada."

"Hiram has a summer place here in the Islands, doesn't he?" I said.

"I think it belongs to his uncle. I've never been there, but he loved to talk about it," she said.

"It's on Wellesley Island, right?" I said.

"Yes, that sounds right," she said.

"Do you know where it is?" Agent Tompkins said, almost coming out of his chair.

"Let me think," she said, again staring off into the distance. "I'll need a minute. But I'm sure it will come to me."

We waited a long time. Eventually, she looked around and appeared almost startled when she realized we were sitting at the table.

"Ivy something," she said.

"Ivy Landing?" I said.

"Yes, that's it. How did you know?"

"You know where it is?" Agent Tompkins said.

"We do," I said.

"We need to get over there," he said.

"Before we eat?" the Chief said.

"Get it to go," the FBI agent said, getting to his feet.

"Hang on," I said, then motioned for him to follow me away from the table.

"What is it?" he said, impatiently tapping his foot.

"We can't leave her by herself," I said. "If she decides to give him a call, he might be gone by the time we get there."

"Call my aunt and ask her to swing by," he said.

I made the call and had a short conversation with Dianne.

"I woke her up," I said. "But she's on her way."

"Okay, then we wait."

We sat back down just as our server returned carrying a large tray. I immediately began wolfing my way through a stack of pancakes. I added a second helping of maple syrup and glanced over at Claudia who had stuffed one end of her napkin down the front of her blouse to serve as a bib. She cut the spaghetti into small pieces with a knife and fork then started eating it with a spoon.

"Would anyone like some?" she said to the table.

We all politely demurred. Dianne entered a few minutes later and sat down next to her former agent.

"Spaghetti and meatballs, huh?" she said. "Breakfast of champions."

"It's good," Claudia said, sounding almost childlike. "Want a bite?"

"No, I think I'll have some eggs," she said, then patted Claudia's hand.

"We need to run," Agent Tompkins said.

"What do you need from me?" Dianne said to her nephew.

"Oh, just sit here and enjoy your breakfast," Agent Tompkins said. "And you should turn your phone off. You know, just so you aren't disturbed." He nodded at Claudia who was thoroughly absorbed with her meal. "Stay off the phone for a while."

"Got it," Dianne said, nodding.

We left them at the table and I glanced back at the mother-child scene playing out. A wave of sympathy for the agent washed over me and I shook my head.

"What's the matter?" the Chief said.

"I feel sorry for her."

"Yeah, I get that. She's running on fumes."

"She scares the crap out of me," Detective Williams said.

"Probably good preparation," Agent Tompkins said. "I have a feeling we're about to meet her male twin."

Chapter 19

If you live long enough, you're bound to meet people facing enormous challenges coping with daily life. Whether driven by genetics or environmental factors, or a combination of both, many individuals, often through no fault of their own, find themselves on the fringe of society trying to deal with their mental maladies while doing everything they can to maintain a façade and convince the people around them, as well as themselves, that everything is hunky-dory.

As someone who dealt with the internal challenges of an overactive mind, I believed I had some understanding of the forces behind Claudia's inexorable slide and swirl down the demon-drain. For whatever reason, I'm able to channel my thought processes and use them to my advantage. However, Claudia's demons appeared to have taken over and, pardon the pun, were now the lunatics running the asylum. Luckily, I had been given an off switch to use when my mind began to run wild. Unfortunately for her, not only had her off switch stopped working, after our encounter with her at breakfast, I had to seriously consider the possibility she had forgotten which room the switch was located in.

These were just a few of the thoughts and questions meandering through my head as the Chief and I drove along Route 12 toward the Thousand Islands bridge that would take us to Wellesley Island. In the end, all I was left with was a genuine and profound sense of sympathy for the 'agent without a clue.'

The Chief turned the music down a bit and glanced over at me.

"You're worried about her, aren't you?"

"Nothing gets past you, Chief," I said, staring out through the windshield. "Aren't you?"

"I am," he said softly. "The whole situation is tragic."

"What do you think is going to happen to her?"

"It depends," he said, checking the rearview mirror. "If she's not involved, maybe she'll head somewhere for a long rest. But if she's part of this, she's likely to go away for a very long time."

"She's not involved," I said, shaking my head. "At least, directly."

"Maybe," he said, turning the music back up.

I listened closely to the sound of Miles' trumpet weaving its way in and out of the intricate, bouncing chord progression being laid down by the piano player.

"This is genius," I said. "Who's on piano?"

"Red Garland," the Chief said as he turned the music up when the piano solo began.

"How do they do it?"

"They practice a lot," he deadpanned.

"Thanks for clearing that up," I said, making a face at him. "What's the name of this track?"

"*Will You Still Be Mine?*"

I flinched in my seat, startling the Chief. He lowered the music then glanced back and forth between me and the road, before finally speaking.

"Talk to me, Suzy."

"That's it," I said. "That's why he did it."

"This oughta be good," he said as he turned off the highway onto the road that would take us to the toll booth.

"He's trying to win her back," I said, turning off the music.

"What on earth are you talking about?"

"He somehow learned that Dianne had fired Claudia," I said, rubbing my forehead. "Maybe he heard the rumor. No, Claudia must have called him after she spotted him at

213

Dianne's presentation. She told him what happened, and he decided to do something to make amends."

"By running Dianne over in the middle of the street?" he said, shaking his head. "Most guys would have just brought flowers."

"Or in his case, candy. Remember who we're dealing with here, Chief," I said, convinced I was on the right track. "Dianne had just given Claudia devastating news. And if Hiram was somehow able to remove the source of her pain, he figured it was the perfect way to win her back. To show how much he loved her."

"That's nuts," the Chief said, coming to a stop at the toll booth. "The guy considered it a *romantic* act?"

"Yeah," I said, giving the attendant a small wave.

The Chief accelerated and we began our ascent up the bridge. I sat back to enjoy the ride.

"How big of a nutjob is this guy to try something like that?" he said.

"Hold that thought," I said, craning my neck out both sides of the vehicle as the sight of the islands appeared far below. In the bright summer sun, the dark blue of the River combined with the emerald of the islands running up and down the channel, and, as always, it took my breath away. "It's so beautiful."

"Yeah," the Chief said, nodding as he looked around. "It never gets old."

"I think Hiram is probably holding on by a thread," I said after we had crested and begun our descent.

"Then he certainly picked the right woman," the Chief said.

"Don't be mean," I whispered.

"Just making an observation," he said, slowing down to make a right turn at the bottom of the bridge on the Wellesley Island side. "I haven't been over here in a while. Ivy Landing is off this road, right?"

"It is," I said, glancing out the back at Detective Williams' car. "You'll see a road sign in a couple of miles."

"How many cottages are there?"

"About a dozen, I think," I said, searching my memory bank. "It's a pretty small inlet."

We made the rest of the drive in silence. The Chief made another right then pulled off to the side of the road next to a stand of pines. We climbed out and stood next to the car waiting for Detective Williams and Agent Tompkins to join us.

"I guess it's time to start knocking on some doors," Detective Williams said, surveying the scene.

"An oldie but a goodie," I said, taking a few steps.

"Hang on," the Chief said. "Where do you think you're going?"

"With the three of you," I said, glancing around at the cops.

All three shook their heads in unison.

"No way, Suzy," the Chief said. "This one is strictly for us."

"Absolutely," Agent Tompkins said. "Civilians aren't invited."

"That's not fair," I said, even though I knew my protests were in vain.

"Just wait in the car," the Chief said. "And stay out of sight. The guy might recognize you from the restaurant and we don't want to spook him."

"Fine," I said, pouting. "But I get to talk to him after you make the arrest."

"Maybe," Detective Williams said.

I watched them head off then climbed back into the passenger seat. I reached into my bag and popped a couple of bite-sized then called my mother.

"Hello, darling. Are you staying safe?"

"Yeah, I'm fine, Mom. I'm here with local, state and federal cops. I think I'll be able to manage. How's Max?"

216

"Adorable," my mother said, laughing. "At the moment, she's on the floor surrounded by all four dogs."

"What are they doing?"

"They're taking turns giving Max a facial," my mother said. "She's probably going to need a bath when they're done. Oh, my. Paulie get a picture of that."

"The dogs are being gentle?"

"Like she's a fragile egg," my mother said. "They're so good with her. What are you up to?"

"I'm sitting in the Chief's car while they go and grab this guy Hiram."

"Good. Make sure you stay there," she said. "What time will you be home?"

"Probably an hour or two," I said, glancing at my watch. "I've been planning on going to the panel this afternoon, but I'm running on no sleep. I might just come home and take a nap."

"Sounds like a good plan," she chirped. "We'll be here. Love you, darling."

"Love you too, Mom."

I was about to call Josie's cell when I remembered she might have gone to bed. I called the main number at the Inn and Jill answered on the first ring.

"Thousand Islands Doggy Inn. How may I help you?"

"Hey, it's me."

"Hi, Suzy. What's going on?"

"If I told you, you probably wouldn't believe me," I said, popping another bite-sized.

"Prior history says otherwise," she said, laughing. "What do you need?"

"Is Josie around?"

"No, she went up to the house. After she managed to add two packs of salt to her coffee, we were finally able to convince her she didn't have her A game this morning. But don't worry, Lacie is keeping a close eye on Velcro."

"How's the dog doing?"

"Well, she's awake, but very disoriented. And I'm sure she's in a lot of pain," Jill said. "The poor thing."

"Yeah, she's been through a lot," I said, stifling a yawn. "Is everything else okay?"

"Things are good," she said. "Are you coming in today?"

"TBD. But I'll check in again later. Thanks, Jill."

"No problem. Have fun."

I tossed the phone in my bag and leaned my head back and closed my eyes. Moments later, I heard the sound of the driver side door opening.

"That was quick," I said, my eyes still shut.

"You. What are you doing here?"

I opened my eyes and stared in disbelief at Hiram who was already sitting behind the wheel.

"Hello, Hiram," I said, baffled by the sight of the disheveled man with the wild-eyed stare.

"You're the one from the restaurant. The one who was grilling me with all those questions."

"I was just making chit-chat," I said, at a loss about what to do next.

"Stupid cop left the keys in the ignition," he said, starting the engine. "Get out of the car."

"You'll get no argument from me," I said, reaching for the door handle.

"No wait," he snapped. "Stay right where you are."

"Whatever you say, Hiram," I said, returning my hand to my lap. I sat in stunned silence as I watched him put the car in reverse then make a wide turn that almost reached the edge of the pines. Eventually, the car bounced back onto the dirt road and we left a trail of dust as he tore toward the highway. "Where are we going, Hiram?"

"For a drive," he said, glancing through the rearview mirror. "Do you think those cops are going to follow us?"

"Rhetorical, right?" I said, glancing over my shoulder. Seeing no sign the cops knew what had just happened, I sunk down into my seat and tried to get control of the thoughts surging through my head. Don't make him mad. Don't make him mad, I chanted silently like a mantra. Eventually, I decided to open with a question.

"Claudia called you, didn't she?"

"Huh?" he said, briefly taking his eyes off the road to glance over at me. "Uh, no."

"It's okay if you tell me, Hiram," I said softly. "She's not going to get in any trouble."

"She's not?"

"She didn't do anything, right?" I said. "You know, apart from giving you a call this morning to tell you the cops were on their way."

"Maybe," he said, his eyes grow wilder by the minute. "You don't think she'll get in trouble?"

"Nah," I said. Apart from being charged with aiding and abetting a murder suspect, I decided. But that was probably a fact I shouldn't share with the guy who was trying to set some sort of speed record. "I'm sure she'll be fine. Can I ask you a question?"

"What?"

"When did Canadians start driving on the left side of the road?"

"Oh, sorry," he said, swerving back into the right lane. "Thanks."

"No problem. But you might want to slow down, Hiram."

"Can't," he said, vigorously shaking his head. "The cops will be right behind us."

"They're not going to shoot you, Hiram," I whispered.

"Why not?"

"Because I'm in the car with you."

"Then I guess I made the right call on bringing you along, huh?" he said, finally taking his foot off the accelerator.

"Yeah, good plan," I said.

"These cop cars handle great," he said, turning the wheel back and forth.

"Easy, Hiram," I said, holding onto my seat as the car began swerving.

"Sweet ride," he said, nodding as he straightened the car and tightened his grip.

"How does it handle compared to the black SUV?" I said, tossing my line into the water.

"You know about that?" he said, glancing over.

"I do," I said, nodding. "And I'm sure I'll never forget it."

Hiram stared out the windshield then exhaled audibly.

"Is the dog dead?"

For a moment, I considered answering in the affirmative, then thought better of it since I had no idea what sort of reaction it might provoke.

"No, she's going to be okay," I said eventually.

"That's good news. Can I ask you a question?" he said, taking another look in his mirrors.

"Well, that's sort of my job, but go ahead."

"I've always wondered something. What is it about people when they see a dog get hurt in a movie?"

"Good question," I said, nodding.

"I mean, you can be watching some sort of shoot 'em up where a hundred people get knocked off and nobody bats an eye. But if a dog gets killed, or even hurt, everyone in the audience loses their mind."

"I know what you mean," I said, keeping a close eye on his movements despite the fact that he appeared to be calming down. "I know whenever one of our dogs is in pain, I usually start bawling like a baby."

"How many dogs do you have?" he said, making solid eye contact for the first time.

"At the moment, seventy-four," I said with a shrug.

"Seventy-four? And they call me nuts."

"After Claudia called you earlier, you decided to hide in the pines?" I said, gently nudging the conversation along.

"Yeah," he whispered. "I should have taken the boat. I don't know what I was thinking."

"Where did you two meet?"

"It doesn't matter," he said, shaking his head.

"It was in an institution, wasn't it?"

"It wasn't an institution," he snapped. "It was better than that. It was our..."

"Sanctuary?" I whispered.

"Yes," he said, almost sounding reverent. "That's exactly what it was."

"But after Claudia got out, she broke things off with you?"

Hiram managed a small nod then looked over at me.

"She broke my heart."

"I'm sorry to hear that, Hiram," I said. "And you thought killing Dianne would somehow make her realize how much you still loved her?"

"That woman pulled the rug out from underneath, Claudia," he said through a violent whisper. "That job was all she had left."

223

"And you know what it's like to lose everything, right?"

"You been reading my file?" he said, his voice developing an edge that made the hairs on the back of my neck stand up.

"No, Hiram," I said, barely above a whisper. "I've just been following the trail of candy wrappers and empty whiskey bottles you've been leaving behind."

"I need to stop drinking," he said to himself more than me. "I get that from my old man."

"Sure, sure."

I dug through my bag. Hiram noticed and reached over and placed a hand over mine.

"What are you doing? You got a gun in there?"

"No, just these," I said, removing a bag of bite-sized. "You want some?"

"Sure," he said, holding his hand out.

We munched chocolate in silence as I sat quietly formulating my next question.

"These are good," he said, holding his hand out for more.

"Much better than that crap candy you've been eating," I said, then focused on him. His stare was still intense, but

224

he now seemed more bewildered than angry. Taking that as a good sign, I pressed on.

"Claudia didn't know you were coming to town, did she?"

"No. I saw an ad for the Arts Festival. As soon as I learned the author was going to be there, I knew Claudia would be with her."

"Did you talk to her after the presentation?"

"Only over the phone," Hiram said, tearing up. "She refuses to meet in person. Says I bring out the worst in her. Can you believe that?"

"I could probably ballpark it," I said with a shrug.

"What?"

"Nothing. Where are we going, Hiram?"

"Canada."

"Okay."

"Do you think the U.S. and Canada have extradition?"

It wasn't the stupidest question I'd ever gotten, but it was a lot like it.

"Yeah, I'm pretty sure they do, Hiram. But that's the least of your problems at the moment."

"Why's that?" he said, turning up the air conditioning. "It's hot in here."

"I hadn't noticed," I said. "Your major problem at the moment is getting through Immigration at the border."

"No problem," he said. "I'll handle all their questions while you just sit there quietly."

"We're in a local cop's car, Hiram. People are going to notice."

He gave it some thought then grinned.

"I'll tell them I'm taking it to a body shop on the Canadian side," he said. "That should work, huh?"

"There's just one small problem," I said.

"What is it?" he said, glancing over with a confused expression.

"There's no damage to the outside of the car."

"Oh," he said, then slowed down and pulled over to the side of the road. "Sit tight. I'll be right back."

I glanced over my shoulder and watched as he got out and violently kicked the side of the car several times. Then he climbed back in and grinned at me.

"Problem solved," he said, kicking up dust and gravel as he accelerated back onto the highway.

"I suppose that might do it," I said. "If I weren't in the car with you."

"Why is that a problem?" he said, glancing over as the car hit seventy.

226

"Because I know everybody who works there," I said, then gave myself a mental pat on the back for coming up with it.

"How is that possible?"

"We throw a party at the restaurant every year for the people who work at Customs and Immigration," I said, lying through my teeth. "As a thank you for all their work keeping us safe."

"Damn," he muttered under his breath. "You think they're going to recognize you, huh?"

"I'd be surprised if they didn't."

Hiram slowed the car and again pulled off to the side of the road. Then he began a three-point turn.

"Change of plans?" I said as I reached into my purse.

"Yeah, we'll cross over further down the River," he said, checking for traffic. "Unless you happen to be on a first name basis with them as well."

"No, I can't say that I am," I said, watching him closely as he put the car in drive and prepared to head back down the stretch of road we'd just come from. "Hiram. Look out!"

"What is it?" he said, turning toward me.

I squirted an enormous dose of Mace directly into his eyes and he screamed in agony. He clawed at his eyes, then tried to do the same to me. But it was no use as the chemical worked its magic. He stomped on the brakes and I lurched forward until my seat belt jerked me back against the seat. Hiram managed to get the car in park before grabbing the bottom of his tee shirt to wipe his eyes.

"What the hell did you do that for?" he said, opening the door and literally falling onto the pavement.

I continued to hold the container of Mace in one hand as I opened the passenger door with the other. I stood behind the car watching Hiram as he crawled around on the blacktop in agony. Moments later, I spotted Detective Williams' vehicle and it came to a screeching stop next to the Chief's car. All three cops scrambled out of the vehicle, their guns drawn and pointed directly at the man on all fours.

"What the heck is the matter with him?" the Chief said, staring in disbelief at Hiram, now rolling around on the blacktop with both hands clawing at his eyes. "What did you do, Suzy?"

I held up the container of Mace.

"That'll do the trick," the Chief said. "Are you okay?"

"I'm fine," I said, tossing the can back into my bag.

"What the hell happened to my car?" he said, scowling at the damage.

228

"Hiram tried to improvise," I said with a shrug. "Unfortunately, he's no Miles."

"I just got that car," he said, glaring at Hiram who continued to wipe at his eyes.

"Don't even think about it, Chief."

"How about I just give him a little love tap?"

"Only if you're into kicking puppies," I said firmly.

"All right," he said, calming a bit. "Since when do you carry around a can of Mace?"

"Ever since Josie made me start during my pregnancy," I said. "You know, just in case."

"Like just in case you happen to get kidnapped by a wingnut?"

"Yeah, something like that," I said, watching as Agent Tompkins and Detective Williams handcuffed Hiram behind his back and not so gently tossed him into the backseat of the detective's car.

I headed back to the Chief's car and climbed in. The Chief hopped in and turned the key before glancing over at me.

"Are you sure you're okay?"

"Yeah, I'm fine," I said through a yawn. "Just exhausted."

"I'll drop you off at home," he said, following the detective's car back toward the bridge.

"No, I want to be there when you guys question him."

"There's no need for that, Suzy. Didn't he already tell you what happened last night with Dianne?"

"Basically," I said, closing my eyes. "But we didn't get a chance to talk about how he managed to smother Selma in her sleep."

"Okay" he said, keeping a close eye on the vehicle directly in front of us. "I don't suppose it would be worth the effort to try and talk you out of it?"

"Why ruin your morning, Chief?" I said with a grin.

He laughed and turned the music up. I listened with my eyes closed and the sound of Miles' trumpet lulled me to sleep. Then a thought floated to the surface, and I opened my eyes and focused on the Chief.

"There's just one more thing."

"Is this the part where you tell me there's no need for your mother to know about this?"

"Great minds think alike."

Chapter 20

I dozed on the drive to the police station and woke when I heard the slamming of car doors. I glanced out the window and spotted the two cops, each holding an elbow, as they lead Hiram inside the ivy-covered building. I followed the Chief and he held the door open for me as I stepped inside and waited for my eyes to adjust to the dim light. He pointed at a chair next to his desk and I slid into it as my eyes threatened to close again.

Hiram, his hands now handcuffed in the front, continued to wipe at his eyes. He gave me a dirty look and I merely shrugged back at him. Agent Tompkins paced back and forth directly in front of Hiram, apparently doing his best to control his anger. Eventually, he sat down but continued to glare at the handcuffed man.

"Can I get something for my eyes?" Hiram said. "Like a gallon of Visine."

"No," Agent Tompkins said.

"We're going to talk for a while, Hiram," Detective Williams said.

"I got nothing to say," Hiram said. "Except for, I want my lawyer."

"You got a lawyer?" Detective Williams said, surprised.

"No."

"We'll let you make some calls in a minute," the detective said. "But we've got a few questions we'd like to ask you first."

"I suppose it can't hurt," Hiram said after giving it some thought. "I already told her everything that happened."

"During the kidnapping, right?" Detective Williams said.

"Kidnapping? We were just going for a little drive," Hiram said, then did his best to focus on me through his bloodshot eyes. "Weren't we?"

I caught the small nod Detective Williams gave me. Playing along in the hope it would get Hiram talking, I looked at the detective and shrugged.

"Yeah, we were," I said. "It's a beautiful day for a drive."

"There you go," Hiram said, rubbing his eyes with his tee shirt.

"A kidnapping charge is the least of your worries," Agent Tompkins said.

Hiram stared down at the floor.

"Why did you try to kill my aunt?"

"Who?" Hiram said.

"My Aunt Dianne."

"She's your aunt?" Hiram said. "I did not know that." He gave the idea some thought then shook his head. "Damn. Trying to kill an FBI agent's aunt probably isn't the smartest thing I've ever done."

"So, you admit you tried to kill her?" Detective Williams said.

"Like I just said, I already told her all about it."

"He thought it was a way to get Claudia back," I said softly.

"What?" Agent Tompkins said.

"I was trying to show her how much I love her," Hiram said.

"That's nuts," Agent Tompkins said, staring in disbelief at the handcuffed man.

"Guilty as charged," Hiram said with a shrug. "When we're done here, I think I should head back to Candlelight. I need a tune-up."

233

"Is that the name of the facility where you met Claudia?" Detective Williams said.

"Yeah. They serve a great fruit cup on Wednesdays," Hiram said.

"Good to know. Where is it located?" the detective said, scribbling a note in his pad.

"Outside of Toronto," Hiram said. "They're really nice there. Canadians, you know," he said with a shrug.

"How did Claudia end up in Canada?" Detective Williams said.

"Good luck finding a place like that in the States," Hiram said. "The government shut down most of the mental health facilities years ago. Did you know that's what created the homeless problem?"

"You don't say," Detective Williams said.

"Yeah, the Canadians are much better at dealing with people like me," Hiram said softly.

"People like you?" Agent Tompkins said.

"Sick people," Hiram said, again rubbing his eyes. "Man, you really got me good. What the hell is wrong with you?"

"Yeah, I'm sorry about that, Hiram," I said, amazed by the way he effortlessly slipped in and out of lucidity.

"I wasn't going to hurt you," he said. "You didn't do anything to Claudia."

"Did Claudia help you?" Detective Williams said, gently probing.

"Claudia? No way. She loves Dianne. I still can't believe she fired her. That was an awful thing to do." Then he focused on me. "Are you sure the dog's okay?"

"She's going to be fine," I said. "What about the garbage bag?"

"What about it?" Hiram said. "After my drive here, the car was a mess."

"But how did you get it in the SUV?" I said.

"What do you mean?" Hiram said, genuinely confused by my question. "I put it there."

"No, I mean, where was it?"

"I cleaned my car, then tossed the bag in the boat when I was ready to head across the River."

"And you left the boat at the state park and walked into town?" Detective Williams said.

"Yeah. It's not that far," Hiram said. "And I like to walk. It clears my head."

"Thank God he's not a couch potato," I whispered.

Detective Williams shot me a dirty look.

"And you carried the bag with you?" the detective said.

"Sure," Hiram said.

"Why on earth would you do that?" the Chief said, baffled.

"I thought I might need it. If anybody had asked me about it, I would have told them I was heading to the laundromat."

"Geez, I guess I overthought that one," I said to myself.

The Chief snorted and shook his head at me.

"How did you know the keys were under the floor mat?" Detective Williams said.

"I was watching the hotel," Hiram said. "I saw the woman put them there."

"And you were still watching the hotel when you saw Dianne and I take the dog for a walk?"

"Yeah," Hiram said. "I figured it was my best chance to take her out."

"You tossed the bag out of the car then parked at the top of the hill?" I said.

"Yup," he said, nodding. "It was pretty clear where you guys were heading. According to Claudia, the writer is big on taking care of the environment. I took a shot she

236

might stop and pick it up. At the time, I thought I'd gotten lucky."

"Until you ran over the dog," I said.

"I'd never hurt an animal," he said. "On purpose, you know."

"But you don't feel the same way about people," Agent Tompkins said, his anger lurking just below the surface.

"No. I don't," Hiram said. "People are a constant disappointment."

Detective Williams stood quietly in the center of the Chief's office, apparently trying to come up with an appropriate response. He glanced around at us and received blank stares in return.

"Okay, Hiram," he said eventually. "Let's shift gears for a moment."

"Your call," he said, again rubbing his eyes. "Geez, what the heck was in that? Drain cleaner?"

"Mace," I whispered as a wave of sadness washed over me.

"Figures," Hiram said. "People hurting people. It never stops."

"Let's talk about the publisher," Detective Williams said.

237

"Who?" Hiram said.

"Selma Blankenship," the detective said.

"Never heard of her."

Detective Williams stared at Hiram for several moments then looked around at us. I leaned forward in my chair and stared hard at the handcuffed man.

"You mentioned her at the Q&A," I said. "Dianne's presentation. Remember?"

"That was a long time ago," Hiram said, frowning. "Who was she?"

"Dianne Harman's publisher," Detective Williams said.

"If you say so," Hiram said with a shrug. "What about her?"

"She's the woman you smothered in her sleep," Detective Williams said.

"I did?"

"Yes," the detective said.

"Look, Detective," Hiram said. "I may slip in and out from time to time, but I think I'd remember that."

"C'mon, Hiram," Agent Tompkins said. "You can tell us."

"I have no idea what you're talking about," Hiram said, then sat back in his chair defiantly with his hands folded in his lap.

I studied him closely, dumbstruck yet convinced he was telling the truth. My neurons that had been silent for the past hour surged and I rubbed my forehead. Detective Williams, at a loss for words, sat down next to the FBI agent and stared off into space.

"You're going to sit there and try to tell us you didn't kill the publisher?" Agent Tompkins said.

"Why would I kill her?" Hiram said, his eyes wide. "I don't even know who the heck she is. Or was. Why do you think I did it?" he said, then his eyes narrowed. "Did she do something to Claudia?"

"Not that we know of," Agent Tompkins whispered.

"So, you drove all the way to Wellesley Island?" I said, unable to control myself.

"I did," Hiram said. "I've got an old Chevy. It's a piece of crap, but it gets me where I need to go."

"We saw the car over at Ivy Landing," Agent Tompkins said. "Which direction did you come from?"

"From Canada," he said. "I drove down then crossed the border near my uncle's cabin. He never uses it."

"You went through Immigration on Wellesley Island?" Detective Williams said.

"Yeah," Hiram said. "I drove from Kapuskasing down to Ottawa, then headed here. I drove all night."

"Kapuskasing?" Agent Tompkins said. "Where the heck is that?"

"In the middle of nowhere," Hiram said. "Just the way I like it."

"Hardly any people, but lots of animals," I said softly.

"You been there?" Hiram said, cocking his head at me.

"No, I haven't."

"Well, you described it perfectly," he said. "I like it there. Except during the winter. I'll go weeks without going outside."

"So, Hiram, when did you cross the border?" Detective Williams said.

"Yesterday. Just before noon. I remember because I was out of food and starving."

"Okay," the detective said. "Did you use a credit card along the way?"

"No," Hiram said, shaking his head. "They're always watching."

"Who's always watching?" Agent Tompkins said.

"People like you," Hiram said, staring at the FBI agent.

240

I stifled a laugh when I caught the look on Agent Tompkins' face. But he took the insult in silence and waited for Detective Williams to continue.

"You must have gone to the bank to get some cash, right?" the detective said.

"That I did," Hiram said. "I stopped at an ATM before I left home and took out five hundred bucks."

"That's easy enough to trace," the Chief said. "And we should be able to get our hands on the video from the border."

"Yeah," Detective Williams said, then got to his feet. "Anybody got any other questions at the moment?"

We all shook our heads and the Chief got to his feet.

"Okay, Hiram. I'm going to take you out back for a while," Chief Abrams said.

"So you can beat me up?"

"Nobody is going to hit you, Hiram," the Chief said.

"Speak for yourself, Chief," Agent Tompkins said, his anger returning as he glared at Hiram.

"Relax," Detective Williams said.

"Good idea. I could use a nap," Hiram said, getting to his feet. "And I'm pretty hungry. You got any of that candy left?"

241

"Here, take the bag," I said, getting up and fishing around for it. I handed the bag to him and he clutched it tight in his fingers.

"Thanks. And for what it's worth, I'm sorry I scared you."

"No harm, no foul, Hiram," I said, flashing him a sad smile.

"I'm ready when you are," he said to the Chief.

We watched the Chief lead Hiram through the door that led to the cells. Then I made a pot of coffee and sat back down as we waited for the Chief to return. When he did, we sat in silence for several moments, each of us alone with our thoughts. Eventually, Agent Tompkins was the first to speak.

"Do you believe him?"

"I do," the Chief said.

"And his story is going to be easy to check," Detective Williams said. "But if he didn't kill the publisher, who the heck did?"

"Before you start talking and say something stupid, my aunt didn't do it," Agent Tompkins said.

"I've moved off that theory," Detective Williams said over the gurgle of the coffeemaker.

"Glad to hear it," Agent Tompkins said, then turned wistful. "You guys ever have to fight the urge to beat the crap out of a suspect?"

"Constantly," Detective Williams said.

"The thought crosses my mind from time to time," the Chief said.

"That would have been like kicking a puppy," I said, glancing at the Chief. "He's obviously a very sick man."

"He's a frigging wingnut," Agent Tompkins said.

"Don't be cruel," I said, glaring at him.

"I can't believe they let him out," the Chief said.

"It's weird," I said. "Sometimes he's in the moment, then he just drifts off."

"Well, if anybody would recognize that, it would be you," the Chief deadpanned.

"Funny."

"Now what?" Detective Williams said as he poured coffee for everyone.

"We dig," Agent Tompkins said.

"Yeah, we dig deep," the Chief said, then looked at me. "You got any ideas?"

"Well, since we're back at square one, I guess the only thing to do is start over."

Chapter 21

After leaving the police station, I dragged myself home, spent a couple of hours playing with Max while chatting with my mom and Paulie, then took a hot shower and fell asleep on my bed while getting dressed. I gave the sleeping Max a final loving gaze then drove back into town. I stood in the doorway of the packed auditorium and eventually spotted Josie sitting near the front. I sat down next to her and she gave me a bemused smile.

"I looked in on you about an hour ago," she said. "I figured you'd be out until dinner."

"No, I'm ready to go," I said, trying to convince myself.

"Since when do you sleep in a bra and one sock?"

"It's been a day," I said through a yawn. I glanced up at the stage where Wilbur and Imelda were sitting behind a table with the other members of the panel on the future of publishing. Dianne was sitting at one end, alone with her thoughts. Joshua Jenkin, a last-minute replacement for Selma, was at the other end beaming out at the audience. Next to him was a woman I didn't recognize. I checked my

244

program and the woman was identified as the CEO of a small publishing house from somewhere in the Midwest.

"This has got major snooze-fest written all over it," Josie said, also reading her program. "What the heck do I care about the future of publishing?"

"You read, don't you?" I said, glancing over at her.

"I also eat hot dogs," she said, returning my stare. "But that doesn't mean I need to sit through a lecture about how they're made."

"Can't argue with your logic," I said with a shrug. "How's Velcro doing?"

"She was awake when I left, but I've got her on some pretty strong painkillers. Lacie is keeping a close eye on her."

"Great job," I said, nodding.

"Where were you this morning?"

"You wouldn't believe me if I told you," I said.

"Try me."

"The cops and I had breakfast with Claudia, then I got kidnapped."

"Fine," she said, swatting me on the knee with her program. "Don't tell me."

I spotted Claudia in the front row. She was disheveled and I made a mental note to ask Dianne how Claudia had

245

managed to slip away long enough to call Hiram and warn him. Then Claudia held both hands up in front of her face and examined her freshly painted nails.

"She's tenacious," I whispered. "I gotta give her that."

"What?" Josie said.

"Nothing. I'm just babbling."

"There's my girl," she said with a laugh then fell silent when the emcee headed for the podium.

I sat through a round of lengthy introductions then the emcee asked each participant to provide the audience with their perspective on where the publishing business was headed over both the short and long term. Wilbur and Imelda went first and they gave a short summary of the changes the industry continued to go through. Then they launched into what I considered to be a well-developed argument about why authors should continue working with a traditional publishing house. As Wilbur went through his list of reasons, Imelda kept glancing down the table at Dianne who was listening closely without making eye contact. When they finished, I had the distinct impression they'd been talking to Dianne instead of the audience. The emcee then asked Dianne for her comments. She leaned forward with both elbows on the table and spoke directly into the microphone. It was impossible to miss the fatigue and stress in her voice.

"Wilbur and Imelda both make excellent points," she said. "And while the traditional publishing route continues to work well for many authors, there are other writers, like myself, who consider the entire publishing industry to be an outdated business model. A dinosaur, if I may be so blunt."

Wilbur and Imelda sat frozen in place with forced smiles, looking like Chef Claire had hit them with her bat. A deathly silence filled the auditorium and the emcee, sensing things were about to go off the rails, did his best to get the conversation back on track.

"I see," the emcee said, checking his notes. "That's a most interesting take."

Wilbur leaned close to his microphone and cleared his throat.

"Let me get his straight," he said, glancing down the table at Dianne. "You're going to keep going with the dinosaur nonsense?"

"We've had this discussion many times, Wilbur," Dianne said, still not making eye contact. "If it walks like a dinosaur, and talks like a dinosaur-"

"Actually," Joshua chimed in from the other end of the table. "I don't think dinosaurs were able to speak."

247

All the members of the panel, along with the audience, stared in disbelief at Joshua. Josie looked over at me with a frown.

"Really?" she said. "What's that old saying?"

"It's better to remain silent and be thought an idiot than to speak and to remove all doubt?"

"Yeah, that's the one," Josie said.

"Hey, Joshua," Imelda said. "Why don't you go take a walk and get lost in the park?"

"There's no need to be rude, Imelda," Joshua said, sitting back and folding his arms across his chest.

Dianne and Wilbur began a testy exchange about indie versus traditional publishing. Back and forth they went and we watched it play out almost as if we were watching a tennis match.

"Geez," I said with a frown. "If this is the argument they have in public, imagine what it's like when they're behind closed doors."

"I can see why Dianne would want out," Josie said, nodding at Wilbur and Imelda. "Those two are a couple of sharks."

"Yeah," I said, closely watching the events unfold on stage. "They certainly are."

"Despite your abhorrence of traditional publishing, an industry that has made you a household name," Wilbur said, puffed up like a male peacock. "I, for one, believe a company like Blankenship adds enormous value in the marketplace."

"I don't abhor it, Wilbur," Dianne said. "It just doesn't work for me anymore."

"Your attitude speaks otherwise," Imelda snapped.

"Then let me be clear," Dianne said, finally focusing on them. "I don't dislike traditional publishing houses. What I abhor…is the two of you."

"Whoa," Josie whispered. "Nice shot. And here I thought this was going to be a snooze fest."

"She's running on a couple hours of sleep," I said, studying Dianne's face. "Her filters are down."

"Well, she might want to put her fists up," Josie said. "Imelda looks ready to throw down."

I nodded and looked over at Claudia who continued to examine her manicure. Then I focused on the panel and felt a touch of sympathy for the emcee who couldn't shake his bewildered stare.

"Despite Dianne's comments to the contrary," Wilbur said, addressing the audience. "The publishing industry is strong, getting stronger by the day, and has considerable room for new companies who are thinking about entering the marketplace."

Imelda beamed at the lawyer and reached over to squeeze his hand. He pulled his hand back as he made eye contact with her and gave her an almost imperceptible shake of his head. She sat back in her chair and folded her hands in her lap.

"Did you see that?" I whispered to Josie.

"See what?"

"Never mind," I said. I glanced around the auditorium then leaned over and whispered to her. "I need to make a quick call. I'll be right back."

"I'll be here," she said, closely monitoring what was happening on stage. "No way I'm missing the rest of this."

I headed out of the auditorium and made the call. Agent Tompkins answered on the first ring.

"Hey," he said. "Did you get some sleep?"

"I did. Not enough, but it was a good start."

"Are you at the panel?"

"I am," I said. "It's fascinating."

"The future of publishing? I'll take your word for it."

"Dianne is getting into it with Wilbur and Imelda," I said.

"On stage? In front of several hundred people?"

"Yeah," I said. "I had no idea how much bad blood had been built up."

"I know she's been under a lot of stress about her contract," Agent Tompkins. "And fighting with Blankenship. But she doesn't like to worry me with the details."

"I need a favor," I said.

"You usually do," he said with a laugh. "What do you need?"

"How long would it take you to find out if any new publishing houses have been registered recently?"

"New companies?" he said. "That's an easy one. I can track that down in an hour at most. Why do you need it?"

"Let's call it a hunch," I said.

"Okay," Agent Tompkins said. "I'll give you a call as soon as I get it."

"Great," I said. "How about we meet at C's? We can have a late lunch."

"Works for me," he said. "I still haven't had a chance to say hi to Chef Claire."

"I don't like your chances. She's still swamped. I'll wait to hear from you," I said. "Oh, one more thing."

"What's that?"

"You still have that file your guys compiled on Selma Blankenship?"

"Actually, I was just sitting here going through it. And some new stuff just came over."

"You mind bringing it with you to the restaurant?"

"As long as you're paying for lunch," he said.

"Later," I said, ending the call and heading back into the auditorium where Dianne and Wilbur continued to go at it. I sat down next to Josie and leaned in close.

"What did I miss?"

"More of the same, basically," Josie said. "Then Joshua tried to jump in and Imelda called him a no-talent hack. He's been pouting ever since."

I looked at the author who was indeed in a snit-fit. If the heated argument between the Blankenship reps and Dianne hadn't been in full swing, I would have found Joshua's mood funny. But it was dwarfed by the heated debate raging at the table.

"This is getting downright nasty," I said.

"Yeah," Josie said, her head still going back and forth like a metronome as the onstage volley continued. "Make sure you ask your mom to schedule another one of these next year."

252

Chapter 22

After the panel discussion finished to a lengthy, albeit somewhat confused, round of applause, Josie and I headed backstage and found Dianne leaning against a pillar looking both depressed and embarrassed. When she saw us heading her way, she forced a small smile and exhaled loudly.

"I'm so sorry," she said.

"For what?" Josie said. "That was fantastic."

"I don't think I've ever behaved that unprofessionally in my life," she said. "The past few days have been a lot to deal with. It finally got to me."

"Don't apologize, Dianne," I said. "From what we heard, they had it coming."

"Their tone took me back to all the meetings we've been having over the past several months. And once I got started, I couldn't stop myself."

"They're both incredibly smug," Josie said.

"I'd like to wring their necks," Dianne said, then paused when she caught the look of surprise on my face. "Metaphorically, speaking, of course."

"Yeah, probably not the best turn of phrase to use given what happened to Selma," I said.

Wilbur and Imelda rushed past on their way out and ignored us as well as the small wave I gave them. Dianne shook her head as she watched them depart through a back door.

"How's Velcro doing?" Dianne said to Josie.

"She's awake. But still confused."

"I'd like to go spend the rest of the day with her," Dianne said.

"Sure, I'm heading back to the Inn. I'll give you a ride," Josie said.

"That reminds me. I need to extend my stay at the hotel."

"No, you can't stay in the hotel that long. That's silly," I said. "Just stay with us at the house. We've got plenty of room."

"That's very kind," she said. "How long will it be before I can take Velcro home?"

"To be on the safe side, I'm thinking a couple of weeks," Josie said. "How are you planning to get back?"

"I haven't even had time to think about it," Dianne said. "That drive would be a tough thing to put her through.

254

But I don't think I could bear the thought of putting her in the cargo area of a plane."

"We can't either," I said. "Fly private. That's how we get our dogs down to Cayman."

"Good idea," she said. "But it's expensive, right?"

"Think of it as an investment," I said, laughing. "That's how we justify it."

"Nothing's too good for the dogs," Josie said. "Are you ready to go?"

"I am," Dianne said.

"Are you heading back?" Josie said to me.

"No, I'm having a late lunch with the cops," I said, then turned to Dianne. "Had Selma been talking about starting another company?"

"Not with me," she said, shaking her head. "But that's not surprising. Our relationship was on pretty shaky ground the last several months. Why?"

"Just a hunch," I said with a shrug. "It's probably nothing." I turned to Josie. "What do you want to do about dinner?"

"I thought I'd grill some steaks," Josie said. "With salad and a loaf of Rustic. You mind picking a couple up at the restaurant?"

255

"You got it," I said. "I'll see you guys later." I started to walk away then turned back to Dianne. "What was that phrase you used to describe them?"

"Bottom-feeding parasites," Dianne said. "Not my finest moment."

"Yeah," Josie deadpanned. "That was an insult to parasites everywhere."

"Are you always like this?" Dianne said, laughing.

"If you believe the rumors," Josie said. "Hey, I still can't find the Connelly book."

"Maybe Captain ate it," I said.

"Nah, crime stories always give him indigestion," Josie said, grinning at Dianne. "I'll be here all week."

"Thanks for the warning," Dianne said.

We walked outside into bright sunlight where a crowd of people were waiting holding copies of Dianne's books. I drove to the restaurant and entered through the kitchen. I found Chef Claire sitting at the chef's table with Charlie, her sous chef, and a couple other staff members. They looked as tired as I felt.

"Hey, you guys taking a well-deserved break?" I said.

"Yeah, we're enjoying the lull before dinner," Chef Claire said. "I can't wait for this festival to be over."

"Sorry to ruin it, but I'm having a late lunch with the cops," I said.

"No problem," Chef Claire said. "Charlie will be happy to take care of you."

"I will, will I?" Charlie said with a laugh.

"I'll make it up to you," Chef Claire said. "I need a nap."

"There's a lot of that going around," I said, heading for the dining room. The three cops were already at the table studying their menus. I plopped down and dropped my bag on the floor. "You missed the fireworks."

"The fireworks are tonight," the Chief said without looking up.

"Funny," I said, reaching for a menu. "Dianne got into it with Wilbur and Imelda during the panel."

"Anything we can use?" Detective Williams said.

"I'm not sure," I said. "But Wilbur and Imelda did show their true colors."

All three cops put their menus down and focused on me. I recounted the story and they listened closely.

"Go back to the part when Imelda grabbed Wilbur's hand and he shook it off," Agent Tompkins said.

"He had just made a comment about how there's always room for new publishing companies," I said. "His reaction, which was sort of a this isn't the time or place response, was what got me thinking."

"Well, your instincts continue to be rock solid," Agent Tompkins said, reaching for a yellow writing tablet. "A new publishing company was registered two months ago."

"In New York?" I said.

"No. San Francisco," the FBI agent said.

"That's probably not helpful," I said with a frown.

"Not so fast," Agent Tompkins said with a grin. "The name of the new company is Wise Publishing." He sat back in his chair and waited for my response.

I came up blank. I shrugged at him.

"I got nothing," I said. "And I'm too tired to guess."

"Wilbur Smithers. Imelda Enconi," Agent Tompkins said.

My neurons reluctantly flickered and I eventually put it together.

"Wise. They used the first initial of their first and last names," I said.

"That's my best guess at the moment," Agent Tompkins said.

"They must have signed something when they registered the company," I said.

"No, their name isn't on it," Agent Tompkins said. "We've got a name and we're trying to run it down."

"That would be a good way to keep your plans quiet," I said.

"Yes, it would," Agent Tompkins said, then spotted our server heading for the table.

"Are you folks ready to order?" she said.

"I think we are, Bobbie," I said.

She took our orders then left the table.

"Did the company filing have any specifics about what type of books they're going to be publishing?" I said.

"No, it was just a general description," the FBI agent said.

"Does Wilbur have a place in San Francisco?" I said, my neurons finally getting their act together.

"No," Agent Tompkins said. "But Imelda does."

"I don't suppose we got lucky enough that the address matches?"

"Oh, we got lucky," he said, nodding.

"Okay, that helps," I said.

"I don't see how," Detective Williams said. "I mean, it's an interesting tidbit, but how does that help us with a motive?"

"I'm not sure it does," I said with a shrug. Then a question surfaced and I focused on Agent Tompkins. "Did you find anything interesting in Selma's journal? You know, the one that was found in the closet?"

"No," Detective Williams said, shaking his head. "All three of us and a couple of my techs went through it and there's really nothing there."

"But it was her daily journal, right?" I said.

"It was," Detective Williams said. "But it reads like she just used it for general reminders and notes to herself."

"It looked like some kind of shorthand," the Chief said, reaching for a piece of bread. "I have no idea why she hid it in the closet."

"Did you bring it with you?" I said.

Agent Tompkins reached into his bag and handed it to me. I started flipping through the pages, working backwards from the most recent date. I gnawed on bread as I read.

"If we're going to focus on Wilbur and Imelda," Detective Williams said. "I still like the love angle as the motive."

"But according to Dianne," I said. "Imelda dumped her for Wilbur. If that's the case, why would they want to kill her?"

"Maybe Selma had something incriminating," Detective Williams said. "Compromising photos. Maybe a sex tape."

"There's just one problem with that," I said. "Since she was Imelda's girlfriend, wouldn't Selma also be in it?"

"Maybe she didn't care," the detective said with a shrug. "The company wasn't doing great. Maybe she thought the publicity would be good for her."

"If she was a wannabe actress, maybe," I said, frowning. "But not a respected publisher from New York." I continued flipping through the journal then landed on an entry that said bonus discussions. "I wish we could get our hands on Blankenship's bank information. You know, revenue entries and outgoing payments."

Agent Tompkins again reached into his bag and tossed a document on the table. I stared at it wide-eyed, then focused on the FBI agent.

"You got it?" I said, stunned.

"Sure," he said with a shrug. "Piece of cake. It just came in. I haven't even had a chance to go through it."

"You guys scare the crap out of me," I said.

"Try not to think about it," the Chief said. "That's the way I deal with it."

"Big Brother is watching," Detective Williams said, getting out of his chair to look over my shoulder.

"Watching?" I said. "He's frigging moved in."

"I thought it might be useful," Agent Tompkins said.

"Did you get the detailed payroll entries?" I said, continuing to flip through the document.

"No, just the summary totals," Agent Tompkins said. "I could get the detail, but it would take a few days."

I continued to study the document. Something was nagging at me, but it wouldn't coalesce. I rubbed my forehead with a deep frown etched into my face.

"Do you smell something burning?" the Chief deadpanned.

"Funny," I said, sitting back in my chair. Then it popped and I flinched, drawing the immediate attention of all three cops.

"It took you long enough," the Chief deadpanned again.

"You're on fire today, Chief." I glanced around the table. "Selma didn't pay bonuses this year."

"I think we're gonna need a bit more," the Chief said.

"All the summary payroll totals are the same," I said. "If she paid bonuses, we'd see a bump in one of the recent entries."

"We would," Agent Tompkins said, reaching for the document.

"Hang on," I said, getting into a brief tug of war with him.

"Well, excuse me," the FBI agent said with a laugh. "I thought you were done with it."

"Their fiscal year ends in June, right?" I said, again absorbed in the document.

"It does," Agent Tompkins said. "If she paid bonuses, it would have been done before the start of the new fiscal year."

"There's nothing here," I said, running a finger down the list of payments. "Hang on. What the heck is this?"

"What?" Agent Tompkins said, leaning in close. "Six hundred and twenty thousand. That's a big check to write."

"It is," I said. "O'Malley Brothers. That ring a bell with anybody?"

All three cops gave it some thought then shook their heads.

"Another easy one," Agent Tompkins said, reaching for his phone. "Hey, Tony. Yeah, I'm good. Just following up on that Blankenship information you sent...Yeah, it was very useful. Thanks for doing that on short notice...I need you to do one more thing. Run a search on a company

263

named O'Malley Brothers. Probably somewhere in or close to the City…No, I'll wait." He held the phone close to his ear and couldn't miss the looks we were giving him. "Hey, it's what we do." He took a sip of water as he continued to wait. "Yeah, I'm still here. Interesting. Thanks, Tony. I'll try not to bug you again."

He set his phone on the table and stared off into the distance, deep in thought.

"What sort of work does O'Malley Brothers do?" Detective Williams said.

"High-end commercial real estate," the FBI agent said as he scratched the stubble on his chin.

"They buy and sell buildings?" the Chief said.

"No, they do renovations to existing space," Agent Tompkins said.

"Maybe Selma's building needed a facelift," the Chief said.

"Yeah, it's possible," Agent Tompkins said, then spotted me grabbing my phone. "Who are you calling?"

"Your aunt."

I put the phone on speaker and set it on the table. Dianne answered on the second ring.

"Hi, Suzy."

264

"Hey. It sounds noisy. Let me guess, you're sitting in Velcro's condo?"

"I am. My poor girl is miserable."

"I'm sure she's very sore," I said. "But she's going to be fine."

"I know. I just hate to see her suffer."

"I'd be surprised if you didn't," I said. "I've got a question for you."

"Sure. Go ahead."

"Had Selma recently done any renovations?"

Dianne laughed for several moments and we waited it out.

"You're talking about the Taj Mahal, right?" Dianne said.

"What?"

"That's what everybody in the office calls it. Her new office. I have no idea how much she spent on it, but from what I hear, it's pretty amazing."

"Six hundred and twenty thousand," I said.

"How do you know that?"

"Your nephew worked his magic. He's here with me."

"Hi, Aunt Dianne," Agent Tompkins said. "So, her new office was a talking point around the office?"

"I imagine it was pretty much all her staff talked about the past few months."

"How did Wilbur and Imelda react to it?" Agent Tompkins said.

"They really didn't share much with me," Dianne said. "Given the strain in our relationship. But I don't think they were very impressed with it."

"Did you know that Selma didn't pay executive bonuses last year?" Agent Tompkins said.

"I did not," she said. "But that would certainly explain the long faces."

"Okay, we'll let you go," Agent Tompkins said. "I'll stop by and see you and Velcro later."

I ended the call just as Bobbie arrived with our food. I took a bite, savored it, then set my fork down.

"Blankenship is a public company, right?" I said.

"It is," Agent Tompkins said.

"I'd love to see who owns the stock," I said.

"The last tab near the back," Agent Tompkins said, through a mouthful of Reuben.

"You guys are unbelievable," I said, shaking my head at him. I studied the page identifying all the major shareholders. "Selma is the largest shareholder, but

266

Wilbur's got a ton as well. There's an R in parentheses next to his name. What does that mean?"

"The stock is probably restricted," Agent Tompkins said.

"English, please," I said with a frown.

"Restricted means just that. His shares have some restrictions about when and how they can be sold."

"Like what?"

"Basically, whatever the board wants to do. Within reason, of course. They still have to comply with SEC regulations."

"Could they put a restriction on Wilbur's shares while he's working there?" I said. "You know, not allow him to sell it."

"Sure. Most stock plans have a vesting period. Which means, while Wilbur has been granted stock options, he has to wait until they vest before he can unload them."

"How long is the vesting period?"

"It's usually four years," Agent Tompkins said. "Companies that use a longer period often have trouble recruiting top talent."

"But you've seen longer?" I said.

"I've seen vesting periods up to ten years," the FBI agent said. "Which really sucks for the executive working under a deal like that. Especially if it was a cliff vesting agreement." He caught the looks we were giving him. "What?"

"Do you really need to ask?" I said.

"Cliff vesting is a 'leave and lose it' plan where the employee only gets control of their stock when it's fully vested. In the ten-year example I came across a few years ago, the executive was awarded ten percent of the stock each year. But if he left before the end of the ten years, he would lose it all and the company could take the stock back."

"Who the heck would sign a deal like that?" Detective Williams said. "It sounds crappy."

"Somebody who needed to go legit in a hurry," I said. "You said the Feebs were about to close in on Wilbur's activities with OC."

"We were," he said. "Huh. How about that? I think you might be on to something here, Suzy."

"How long has Wilbur been working at Blankenship?" I said.

"A little over three years. Son of a gun."

"Now that Selma is out of the way, what's the chance that Blankenship is ripe to be acquired?" I said.

"I'd say the chances are pretty good," Agent Tompkins said. "There's a lot of consolidation still going on in the publishing industry."

"But what difference would it make if the company was acquired by somebody else?" the Chief said. "Wilbur's still only been there three years."

"Lots of side deals are cut during acquisitions," Agent Tompkins said. "And given the size of that deal, paying Wilbur full price for all his stock would be a rounding error."

"And since Wilbur is Blankenship's lead counsel, he'd probably be leading the negotiations," I said.

"Yeah, I imagine he would," Agent Tompkins said. "And he and Imelda could cash out their stock and use the money to fund their new company." He stared at me for a long time before speaking. "Suzy, you continue to amaze me."

I felt my face turn red and mumbled a thank you.

"Now what?" the Chief said. "Identifying them is one thing. Catching them is something else altogether."

"They killed that woman over some stock options?" Detective Williams said. "We have to put them away for a very long time. You know, throw the book at them."

"Throw the book at them?" the Chief said, frowning at the detective. "Really? That's the best you got?"

"I've been watching a lot of Dragnet reruns," Detective Williams said.

I listened to their exchange with a smile and resumed eating. Then I sat back in my chair.

"The book. Son of a gun."

"What is it now?" the Chief said.

I grabbed my phone and called the hotel.

"Hi, George. It's Suzy…Yeah, Max is great. Thanks for asking. Hey, I was wondering if your staff happened to find a book in Selma Blankenship's room the other day…Yeah, Michael Connelly. That's the one…No, I'll swing by and pick it up…Hang on. Can you do me a favor? Put the book back where you found it…Should you ask why? No, probably not."

I set my phone down and took a big bite of my sandwich. I savored it then wiped my mouth. I caught the confused looks on all three cops faces and beamed at them.

"Don't let me forget. We need to stop by the hotel after lunch."

Chapter 23

We entered the hotel lobby and I waved George over. He came out from behind the registration desk and approached with a confused look on his face. After returning our perfunctory greetings, he focused on me with a laser-like stare.

"Suzy, what the heck is going on?" he said, rocking back and forth on his heels.

I glanced around at the three cops and Detective Williams nodded for me to continue.

"We think we've had a breakthrough about who killed the Blankenship woman," I said.

"Easy, Suzy. Let's call it a working theory for now," Detective Williams said.

"Tomato, tomahto," I said with a shrug.

"Don't start," the Chief said, gently squeezing my arm.

"Who's the suspect?" George said.

When no one responded, George folded his arms across his chest, obviously annoyed.

"Suzy, Chief, we go way back. And this is still my hotel. I think I have a right to know what's going around here."

I deferred to the cops and Agent Tompkins was the first to speak.

"We'd like to speak with Wilbur Smithers and Imelda Enconi," the FBI agent said. "They're still here, right?"

"They are," George said. "They got back about an hour ago. But they're getting ready to check out." He stared off for a moment. "Yeah, I can see them doing it. I don't like their attitude. They come across as if they're doing me a favor staying here."

"Like I said, it's only a working theory at the moment," Detective Williams said.

"And like I said," I muttered under my breath. "Tomato, tomahto." Then I felt a pinch and jerked my arm back. "Ow. Hey, that hurt."

"It's supposed to hurt," the Chief said, raising an eyebrow at me. "Knock it off."

"Are they sharing a room?" Agent Tompkins said.

"They are," George said. "The Captain's Quarters suite."

"That's the one right next to the one Selma was in," I said. "But they weren't staying there the night she was killed."

"No, but the couple who was staying there checked out as soon as they heard what happened to the Blankenship woman," George said. "They're the two best suites in the hotel. And as soon as those two realized that, they wanted it. It makes sense. You can't beat the view."

"Were you able to put the book back?" I said.

"I did it myself," he said, nodding. "How is it?"

"The new Connelly?" I said.

"Yeah."

"It's great. As always," I said. "I'll lend it you just as soon as we finish it."

"No hurry. I won't have time to read until after Labor Day." He handed me a keycard. "You'll need this to get in."

"Is there anybody staying there at the moment?" the Chief said.

"Not until you take down all that yellow tape," George said.

"It won't be long," Detective Williams said.

"I certainly hope not," George said, annoyed again. "It's high season and I'm leaving a lot of money on the table."

"We appreciate your patience, George," the Chief said.

"Who should I call if I hear gunfire?" George said, sounding half-serious.

"You call us," Chief Abrams deadpanned.

"Thanks for clearing that up, Chief. Okay, I need to run. We've got a lot of guests checking out. I need to give my folks a hand."

"Thanks, George," I said. "Stop by the restaurant. I'll buy you dinner."

"Finally, an idea I can get behind," he said, then gave us an over the shoulder wave as he headed back to registration.

We continued to stand in the middle of the lobby in a small huddle.

"How do you want to do this?" the Chief said.

"Well, I need to go up to get the book," I said. "And get them talking."

"Not by yourself, you're not," the Chief said. "At least one of us is going with you."

"I'll go," Agent Tompkins said.

"They won't talk with a cop in the room," I said.

274

"Then I'll have to figure out somewhere to hide, won't I?" the FBI agent said.

"We'll figure something out," I said with a shrug.

"I'll stay out in the parking lot," Detective Williams said. "They're probably going to hit the road right after they check out. I'll do my best to get them talking, but we've got nothing to hold them on. As soon as they're ready, I'm going to have to let them go."

"Yeah, you're right," Agent Tompkins said. "What's the matter, Chief?"

"I'm just wondering if they might decide to leave by boat," the Chief said. "I doubt if they're suspicious, but you never know."

"Where the heck would they get a boat?" Agent Tompkins said.

"There are tons of rental places in town," he said.

"It sounds like a longshot, Chief," Detective Williams said.

"It is," the Chief said. "But it'll give me something to do. And I can enjoy the view of the River while I'm doing it."

"Knock yourself out," Agent Tompkins said. "Okay, wish us luck." He pressed the up button. "You ready to do this?"

"I am," I said, entering the empty elevator and leaning against the back wall.

"What's the plan?" Agent Tompkins said.

"Well, plan might be a bit of a stretch at the moment. But I thought we might be able to use some of the information we talked about at lunch."

"And you think they're just going to confess?"

"Maybe. If I make them mad enough."

"Suzy, you gotta promise not to do anything stupid. There's a very good chance they killed Blankenship, and I doubt if they'd hesitate to do it again."

"But how could they do that and not get caught?" I said.

"Don't forget Wilbur worked in OC for years," Agent Tompkins said. "I'm sure he could come up with something."

"Relax, Agent Tompkins," I said. "Apart from tossing me off the balcony, I don't see anything they could get away with."

"Off the balcony?" he said, giving it some thought. "That would certainly do the trick. Or they could kidnap you and drive off with you stuffed in the backseat."

"Twice in one day?" I deadpanned. "That would have to be some sort of world record."

"Yeah, I'll call Guinness," he said, ignoring my levity.

"Detective Williams is waiting by their car," I said. "Kidnapping wouldn't work."

"Just promise to be careful with them, okay?"

"Sure, sure."

The elevator came to a stop on the top floor, and we headed down the long hallway. I inserted the keycard and we stepped inside the suite. George was right. There were sections of the suite cordoned off with yellow tape, and I had to walk around it or duck underneath in a couple of places. I motioned for Agent Tompkins to stay inside as I stepped out onto the balcony. A gentle breeze wafted over me and I took a few moments to enjoy the spectacular view. Then I leaned over the balcony and looked down at the water directly underneath me.

"What are you doing?" Agent Tompkins said from the doorway.

I turned and held a finger to my lips to shush him then spotted the book sitting on a small table. I picked it up then focused on the balcony to my right. A four-foot gap separated the two balconies and I heard the sound of metal scraping against tile. I spotted Imelda stretched out in a lounge chair. It appeared like she might be taking a nap, but it was impossible to tell given the dark sunglasses she was wearing. The only other thing she was wearing was a small two-piece bathing suit, and I stared in amazement at her set of washboard abs. I poked a finger into my belly and realized that it was definitely time to take Chef Claire up on her offer to put together a training regimen for me.

I coughed softly, then faked a stifled sneeze but I got no reaction from the woman on the other balcony. Then I dropped the book and it landed with a solid thump. Imelda glanced around then sat up and spotted me.

"I'm so sorry," I said, bending down to pick the book up. "I'm such a klutz."

"Suzy? What the heck are you doing over there?" Imelda said, getting up out of her chair.

"I left this here the other day," I said, holding up the novel. "Fortunately, the staff just left it after they found it."

"Is that the new Connelly?" she said.

"It is. It's great."

"I just wish he was one of our writers," Imelda said. "Cha-ching, right?"

"Yeah," I said, laughing along with her. "You guys staying another night?"

"No, we're leaving soon. I'm just relaxing for a bit while Wilbur packs," Imelda said. "How is Dianne's dog doing?"

"She's going to be fine," I said.

"Good," she said, apparently out of things to say. "Well, thanks again for inviting us to the festival."

"Maybe you guys can come back next year," I said.

She flashed a crocodile smile and shook her head. "Doubtful."

"Yeah, I get that," I said, going for chatty. "It's certainly nothing like New York up here. Say, I was wondering if you have a few minutes to chat?"

"Isn't that what we're doing?"

Since she hadn't removed her sunglasses, it was impossible to read her eyes. But her voice sounded cautious, almost guarded.

"I have a few questions about the publishing industry," I said.

"Okay. Go ahead."

"Well, I've been thinking about trying to write for a long time, and I think I'm ready to get started. And I have a great idea for a book."

"Really?" she said. "Fiction or non-fiction?"

"I guess that depends on how things play out," I said to myself more than her.

"What?"

"Nothing. I'm just babbling. Definitely fiction."

"Interesting. Well, we're always on the lookout for new talent. And this is a good time to talk to us."

"Why's that?"

"We're about to…expand our acquisition efforts," she said. "Go ahead. Give me your best pitch."

"That's very generous of you, Imelda," I said, pursing my lips tight as I got ready to toss my line into the water. "Would you mind if I came over there? I'd probably do a better job if we were in the same room."

She gave it some thought then nodded.

"Sure, I've got a few minutes. Come on over."

"I'll be right there," I said, tossing the book into my bag and heading inside. Agent Tompkins was standing behind the curtain and nodding at me. "Were you able to hear all that?"

"I was. Well done."

"Thanks," I said. "Did you bring a recording device with you?"

"No, it completely slipped my mind," he said, giving me a blank stare.

"This is not the time to get snarky, Agent Tompkins," I said. "I'll figure out a way to get them on the balcony. Will that thing be able to pick up our conversation?"

"Ten feet? Yeah, I like my chances," he said.

"Did you bring that attitude with you to the Bureau or do they train you to be like that?"

"You want to stand here and fight, or would you like to see if we can catch a couple of killers?" he said.

"Fair enough," I said. "There's a lounger near the railing I think you'll be able to hide behind."

"That should work."

"And I know you brought you gun with you," I said.

"Your point being?" he said.

"Just that you've got everything you need. Some to record with. Something to shoot them with if things head south."

"Suzy, don't even joke about that," he whispered. "But if something does happen, drop to the ground and make yourself as small as possible.

Subconsciously, I poked my belly then gave him a small shrug.

"I'll do my best."

Chapter 24

I knocked softly and Wilbur opened the door and waved me in.

"Hi, Suzy. What's a nice surprise. Come on in."

"Hi, Wilbur. You guys are hitting the road?"

"We are. But we have some time. Imelda says you have a pitch for us."

"I do," I said. "At least I think I do. I've never done one before."

"Just take it one step at a time and you'll do fine," he said, gesturing toward the balcony. "You guys go ahead and get started. I'll join you as soon as I finish packing."

I headed outside on the balcony, identical to the one I'd just left, and found Imelda standing with her back against the railing next to a small table and chairs set. I fixated on her rippled abdomen again and shook my head in disbelief.

"Can I ask you a question?" I said.

"Sure."

"When's the last time you met a carbohydrate?"

282

Imelda laughed as she sat down and motioned for me to join her.

"You're funny. Take my advice. Try to incorporate that into your writing. To answer your question, I do my best to avoid carbs," she said. "But I must admit I had a hard time saying no to that rustic Italian you serve at the restaurant."

"But you must also work out, right?"

"Like a crazy person," she said, removing her sunglasses. "It's how I deal with all the stress."

"That's a lot of stress," I said, then caught the look she was giving me. "I meant that as a compliment."

"Got it," she said, draping a leg over her knee. "I was an athlete when I was a kid. And I ended up with a lot of colleges bidding for my services. I almost took a swimming and diving scholarship at Texas, but I decided to focus on gymnastics. So, I accepted the offer from Georgia."

"Nice," I said, genuinely impressed.

"It was fun," she said. "And it saved my parents a boatload of money." She lit a cigarette and noticed my surprised look. "I know, it's a dreadful habit. But it also helps keep the weight off. Now, tell me all about this book."

"Well, I must admit that I'll be stealing a lot from the events of the past few days," I said.

"Rule number one," she said, exhaling smoke skyward. "Amateurs steal, professionals borrow."

"Interesting," I said, nodding.

"All the stories have been told. The secret is telling yours in a new way. Just change the names of the people and places and you'll be fine. So, what's the storyline?"

"It's about the murder of a woman who owns a major publishing house," I said.

"Topical, if nothing else," she said, easing into her publishing role. "Now that I think about it, it would make a good story. So, it's a murder mystery?"

"Yes."

"There's always a market for them. If they're any good."

"As opposed to Joshua's books?"

"Poor Joshua," she said with a chuckle. "He started out with so much promise. But I'm afraid he's lost his magic. Tell me more."

"Well, there would be several potential suspects. A couple of writers, some of the people who work for the publishing company. And a lawyer."

"Lawyers always make good villains," she said, taking a long drag on her cigarette. "How does the woman die?"

"Well, I was thinking about having her smothered in her sleep, but that would be a blatant steal. So, I think I'll have her stabbed."

"That works," she said, nodding. "A little messy, but silent. It wouldn't attract a lot of attention in case there are any bystanders. You know, potential witnesses."

"That's what I thought," I said.

"So, what's the hook?" Imelda said, crushing her cigarette out.

"It ends up being an inside job. She's killed by someone who works for her."

"I see," Imelda said, fiddling with her pack of smokes. "What's the motive?"

"Well, if I can manage to pull it off, it will be a combination of money and revenge."

"Revenge?" she said, giving in and reaching for another cigarette. "How so?"

"A bad breakup," I said. "The woman who runs the publishing house gets dumped by her girlfriend. And her ex starts dating someone else who works there."

"I see," she said, exhaling smoke. "Who?"

"It should probably be the lawyer, right?" I said. "You know, since he's the primary villain, it would keep the story tighter if he's the one involved with the publisher's ex-girlfriend. Don't you think?"

The penny dropped for her and her expression morphed into a narrow-eyed stare.

"It's your book," she said with a shrug. Then she spotted Wilbur leaning against the doorjamb. "There you are. You need to hear this. Suzy has a very interesting idea for a murder mystery."

"Don't worry, I've been listening," Wilbur said. He forced a small smile, and I couldn't miss the veins pulsing around his temples. "Please, continue."

"The major reveal," I said, then paused. "That's the right term for it, isn't it?"

"It is," Imelda said.

"The reveal revolves around the money part of the motive. The villain, the lawyer, has a ton of stock options but wants to get out to start a new publishing company with his girlfriend. But the problem is that the stock is restricted. It's a type of stock deal where the employee gets nothing if he leaves the company before the vesting period runs to completion."

"Yes, I've heard of them," Wilbur said. "I think you might be onto something, Suzy."

"Oh, I'm so glad to hear that," I said, leaning back in my chair and closely studying their expressions.

"Yes, I think we can do something with this one, Wilbur," Imelda said. "If you'll excuse us, Suzy, we're going to have a quick chat about a potential offer."

"Right now?" I said.

"We've found it's always better to strike while the iron is hot," Wilbur said. "If you'll excuse the hackneyed metaphor."

"This is so exciting," I said.

"Hold that thought," Wilbur said with a tight grin as he motioned Imelda to follow him inside.

After they were out of sight, I glanced over at the next-door balcony and spotted Agent Tompkins' head peering around the lounge chair he was hunched down behind. He waved me away and I headed for the glass doors and stood out of sight as I tried to listen in on their hushed conversation. The conversation was muffled and I glanced around the balcony. On the table, I spotted a drinking glass and grabbed it. Hidden behind the partially closed curtains, I held the glass up to one of the doors and pressed an ear tight.

287

"Huh, how about that?" I grunted moments later. "It actually works."

"You need to relax, Imelda," Wilbur said softly.

"She knows," Imelda whispered violently.

"I'm aware of that," Wilbur said. "I was listening, remember?"

"What do we do?"

"Nothing. They don't have any proof," Wilbur whispered.

"I'm freaking out, Wilbur," Imelda said. "And the dog lady has been hanging out with that FBI agent and the other cops."

"Relax, Imelda," Wilbur said. "Look, I'm going to load the car. You go out there and offer her a chunk of money for the book. Then tell her she can't talk to anybody about the book or the deal's off. We'll figure out a way to get her to keep her mouth shut."

"How are we going to do that?" Imelda said, her voice rising.

"How the hell do I know?" Wilbur snapped. "We'll get to that later. Just don't do anything stupid like you did the other night."

"It was your idea," she said.

"Yeah, but I didn't tell you to kill Selma while she was right down the hall," Wilbur said.

"So, now it's on me, huh?" Imelda said. "That's the way you're going to play it?"

"I'm not playing anything. I'm just telling you to relax. Offer her the deal to buy us some time, then if this thing continues to heat up, we'll fly somewhere where they'll never find us."

"Good plan, Wilbur," Imelda said in a mocking tone.

"You got a better idea?

"I do," she said coldly.

"Please, Imelda. Don't do anything crazy."

"Just go load the car. I'll be down in a minute."

I felt the hairs on the back of my neck tingle and I headed to the other side of the balcony and stood with my back against it. I glanced over at the other balcony and couldn't miss the gun in Agent Tompkins' hand.

"I probably should have thought this one through a bit more," I whispered aloud to myself.

"I've got great news, Suzy," Imelda said, remaining in the doorway. "We'd like to make you an offer for the book."

"You would?" I said. "That's great."

"We usually don't give new authors much of an advance," she said. "But we think you have something special to offer. How does a hundred thousand sound?"

"Not as good as two," I said with a shrug.

"You want two hundred thousand?" she said, surprised.

"Nah, a hundred would be fine," I said. "I'm not doing this for the money."

"What other earthly reason could you have besides money?" she said, genuinely surprised.

"I'm into justice," I said softly.

"I see," she said, her expression morphing into a dark and dangerous stare.

"Can I ask you a question?"

"We really need to hit the road," she said. "But go ahead."

"Did Selma figure out what you and Wilbur were up to before or after you kicked her out of your bed?"

Imelda flinched before a calm seemed to come over her. She gave me a crocodile smile and put her hands on her hips as she stared me down.

"And Selma couldn't resist the other night when you knocked on her door," I said. "What did you do, Imelda? Promise her a reconciliation?"

"You're a smart woman," she said eventually.

"Thanks. I have my moments. It was the problem with Wilbur's stock wasn't it?"

"Among other things," Imelda said. "But that was the major problem. And Selma was making our lives very difficult."

"A control freak who was scared to death about losing control," I said, nodding.

"Exactly."

"So, Selma started surrounding herself in luxury. Probably to prop herself up, right? An attempt to bolster her self-confidence?"

Imelda maintained a small smile but said nothing.

"And when she didn't pay you guys your bonus, that was the last straw."

"How on earth do you know that?" she said, baffled.

"I had a lot of help," I said, sneaking a quick peek at Agent Tompkins who was now facing us in a kneeling position with his gun directly pointed at Imelda. "What do we do now, Imelda?"

"You sign the deal and agree to keep your mouth shut," she said. "Or Wilbur and I take off and roll the dice. Maybe even take more drastic measures. Wilbur still has a lot of friends from his former line of work."

"I don't want the deal," I said, fighting the lump forming in my throat. "I have no intention of writing all this crap down. The whole thing makes me sick to my stomach."

"Okay," she whispered, then glanced out at the River. "My, that's a big ship. I don't recognize the flag. What country is that?"

The next few seconds would play in my head on a loop for the next several days.

I turned around to take a look in the direction Imelda was pointing, then heard the padding of bare feet on tile just as Agent Tompkins yelled.

"Suzy, get down!"

I did as he commanded just as Imelda caught a glimpse of Agent Tompkins out of the corner of her eye. But before she could regain her bearings, she ran into me at full speed and her knees bounced hard off my butt. She was launched into the air, then landed and teetered on the top of the wrought iron before toppling over the balcony. I clamored to my feet and watched her descent. As she continued to drop, her scream drifted skyward. She hit the water with a perfect belly flop, disappeared from sight, then floated to the surface on her back. I shook my head as I continued to stare down at her lifeless body.

"You probably should have taken the diving scholarship," I whispered.

"Are you okay?" Agent Tompkins said, sliding his gun back into its holster.

"I'm fine. Thanks."

Agent Tompkins removed his phone from his pocket and made a call. As he waited, he peered over the edge of his balcony at Imelda who was beginning to drift downriver in the current. "Is she alive?"

"I'm not sure," I said, taking another look down. "She hit the water hard."

"Seventy feet will do that," he said, taking another look down before focusing on his phone. "Hey, it's me. Do you see Wilbur down there?" He listened for a few moments then continued. "Good. Go ahead and arrest him…Yeah, she got it out of her."

Agent Tompkins put his phone away and took another look over at the balcony.

"I think I've seen enough crazy the past few days to last me a long time," he said.

"I know I've had my fill." Then I leaned over the balcony and called out. "Hey, Chief."

"Yeah," he responded. "Is everything okay up there?"

"We're fine," I said. "I can't see you. You on the dock?"

"I am."

"Is she alive?"

"Yeah, I see some twitching."

"The current has got her. Can you fish her out?"

"The things I do for this job," he said. "Hang on. I need to take my shoes off."

"Cool. We'll be right down."

We exited the hotel through the front door and spotted Detective Williams leading the handcuffed Wilbur to the police car. I did my best lumber to keep up with the FBI agent's brisk pace as we headed down the walkway than ran along the side until we came to the long wooden dock that fronted the hotel. When we reached the Chief, he was in the water holding onto the dock with one hand and Imelda with the other.

"Give me a hand getting her out of," he said.

"Hang on," I said, kneeling over the edge and adjusting Imelda's two-piece back in place.

"Thanks," she managed to mumble before letting loose with a loud groan as the three of us pulled her out of the water and placed her on the dock. "I think I broke some ribs."

"Just lie still until the ambulance gets here," I said.

"You have no proof," she whispered. "You do know that, don't you?"

"I'm sure the lawyers will sort it all out," I said. "Can I ask you a question?"

"It's not like I have a vote at the moment. What now?"

"Why the heck did you try to push me off the balcony? All that would do is compound your problems."

"Who's to say you didn't fall?" she said softly then groaned again. "Where's Wilbur?"

"He's in the back of a police car," Agent Tompkins said.

"This whole thing was his idea," she said, clutching her ribs as she tried to catch her breath.

"I really don't care, Imelda," the Chief said.

"Harsh," I said, glancing over at him.

"Well, I don't," he said.

I let it go and focused on Imelda. Her breathing continued to be labored, and I couldn't miss the discoloration already forming on her face.

"Did you really like the book idea or were you just blowing smoke?"

"No, it would make a good story. But good ideas are a dime a dozen," she said, doing her best to focus on me. "It's all about execution."

I nodded then took a step back when I spotted two paramedics trotting down the dock rolling a stretcher. We watched as they examined her then strapped her to the device. Moments later, she was on her way to the hospital where I was sure she'd be handcuffed to the bed until she was well enough to be charged and put on trial.

"What do you think?" I said to Agent Tompkins.

"If the charges will stick?"

"Yeah."

"It's not our case," he said. "But I'll make sure Detective Williams gets everything he needs."

"They'll be able to afford the best lawyers," I said.

"And so will Blankenship Publishing. I hope your local DA is up to it," Agent Tompkins said. "Let them fight it out."

"Don't you care?" I said, surprised by his comment.

"Of course, I do," he said, staring out at the River. "But I don't try them. I just catch them."

"Staying in your lane, right?"

The three of us began a slow walk down the dock toward the path that would take us to our cars.

296

"It took me a long time," Agent Tompkins said. "But when I finally figured out the key to my success, I became a much happier man."

"This I gotta hear," I said with a laugh.

"The secret to being good at everything you do in life is to only do things you're good at."

I gave it some thought then nodded.

"Hey, that's pretty good advice. You're a smart guy, Agent Tompkins."

He gave me a small smile and a gentle punch on the shoulder without breaking stride.

"Nothing gets past you."

Epilogue

I gently bounced Max on my knee and she giggled with delight. The house dogs were hovering next to the couch keeping a close eye on both me and the baby. Dianne was sitting across from me watching the scene play out with an enormous smile. Velcro was curled up at her feet still bandaged around the ribs and wearing an elaborate harness designed to keep her hip in place.

"She's a great kid," Dianne said. "You did well."

"Thanks," I said, taking a break from the bouncing to wipe the drool off Max's face. "She's something else, that's for sure."

"It's such a pity her father isn't here to see this," she said, then stopped short, embarrassed by the comment. "I'm sorry. I shouldn't have brought that up."

"Don't worry about it," I said, holding Max close to my chest as I teared up and choked back a wave of emotion. "Most times it comes and goes without any help from anybody else."

"Still, I shouldn't have said anything."

"It's okay," I said, setting Max back down on my knee. "But right after our adventure in the middle of the street, it was pretty bad for the next few days."

"Because it reminded you of your husband's accident?"

"The sound, primarily," I said. "That sickening thud I heard when the SUV ran over Velcro. That's what brought it all back."

Josie and Chef Claire returned from the kitchen with a tray of appetizers. The house dogs immediately went on point.

"Not a chance," Josie said to them. "In fact, I think we'll put you guys outside for a while. It's a beautiful day." She started to head back to the kitchen before realizing she was travelling solo. "Let's go guys. Captain…I'm talking to you."

The Newfie snorted but reluctantly followed her, trailed by Chloe and Chef Claire's Goldens. Moments later, she returned and plopped down on a couch.

"I love Saturdays," she said, stretching out with her hands behind her head. Then she sat up abruptly. "Velcro. If you keep chewing at that harness, I'm going to get the cone. And you know how much you love that."

299

The Vizsla cocked her head at Josie then rested it on her front paws.

"Good girl," Josie said. "Hey, I forgot to ask. What's happening with Claudia?"

"She's back home," Dianne said, then paused before continuing. "I hired her back."

"As your agent?" I said, surprised.

"No. I'm afraid her days of being out among the public are over."

"Good call," Josie said. "What's she going to be doing?"

"She's handling some things for me behind the scenes. It's more of a personal assistant role."

"That was very nice of you," I said.

"She always did her best," Dianne said. "And I should have realized how much trouble she was in a lot earlier."

"Has Detective Williams updated you on what's happening with the rest of them?" Josie said.

"They're still trying to figure out what to do with Hiram," I said. "He's been charged, but Detective Williams thinks his lawyer might be able to convince the judge he's not stable enough to stand trial."

"An insanity plea," Josie said with a shrug. "Not much of a stretch."

"No, it certainly gets my vote," I said. "Detective Williams says there a good chance Hiram will end up back in Canada at a facility designed to deal with people like him," I said. "And Imelda and Wilbur have both lawyered up. And what is really interesting is they're using different lawyers."

"Let me guess," Josie said. "They're going to take turns throwing each other under the bus."

"That's what it looks like," I said, cleaning Max's drool away with a wet wipe.

"You got them on tape," Josie said. "How hard can it be to get a conviction?"

"I have no idea," I said with a shrug. "But Wilbur and Imelda are both spending several hundred dollars an hour to find out."

"Have you heard from the Blankenship board yet?" Josie said.

"I did. I'm officially released from my contract at the end of the month," Dianne said. "They want all of this to go away as soon as possible. And then it's full speed ahead." She focused on me. "Have you given any more thought to my offer?"

"I have," I said softly. "And I appreciate it. But I'm going to pass."

"Can I ask you why?" she said, reaching down to stroke the Vizsla's head.

"It was something your nephew said."

"Since when do you listen to the cops?" Josie said with a laugh.

"Funny," I said, making a face at her. "He was talking about his secret to success."

"The key to being good at everything you do is to only do things you're good at," Dianne said. "I've heard that one a lot from him."

"It's pretty good," I said. "And when I thought about it, I realized he's probably right. At least when it comes to the idea of me being a writer."

"It would take time, but I'm sure you could get good at it," Dianne said.

"Nah, I'll leave that people like you," I said, patting her knee. "Between Max and the dogs, I've got more than enough to keep me busy."

"Do you mind if I steal some of your ideas for the mobile grooming service series?"

"Don't you mean borrow?" I said with a grin.

"Yes, that's exactly what I mean," she said, laughing.

My phone buzzed and I checked the number.

"Hey, Rooster. Yeah, she's ready to go. See you in a bit." I hung up and looked at Dianne. "Rooster's on his way."

"Okay," she said, getting to her feet. "Thank you for your hospitality. You were right. It was so much better than the hotel."

"You're always welcome. Maybe we can do it again next year."

Dianne frowned at me.

"I'll need to give that one some serious thought."

Josie snorted as she got off the couch and grabbed the handle of Dianne's suitcase. She wheeled it toward the kitchen and we followed. Velcro struggled a bit walking with the harness but it was obvious she was definitely on her way to making a full recovery. We walked down to the driveway and waited for Rooster.

"It's a beautiful day," Dianne said, glancing out over the bay. "You should take the boat out."

"No, it's a house day," I said. "And Max isn't ready for the River yet. But next summer, right, Max?"

Max kicked her legs excitedly then spit up on my tee shirt.

"She gets that from her mother," Josie deadpanned.

"Thanks, Max," I said, handing her to Josie while I wiped it off my tee shirt. Then I held out my arms and Josie handed her back. I held her in the crook of my arm and waved to Rooster when he pulled into the driveway. He hopped out and Josie tossed him the keys to the van we used to transport dogs.

"Good morning," he said, heading straight for the baby. "Hello, Max." He tickled the bottom of her feet and she giggled with delight. "You ready to go?"

"I am," Dianne said, taking a final look out over the water. Then she pulled me in close for a hug. "Thank you so much, Suzy."

"You're very welcome. It's been memorable."

Dianne grabbed Josie by the shoulders and gave her an extended, bone crushing embrace.

"Thank you so much for saving Velcro," she said, then let go and brushed back a tear.

"She did most of the work," Josie said, grimacing from the hug. Then she turned to Rooster. "You'll need to carry her up the steps when you get to the plane. And be careful of that hip."

"Will do," he said. "Is the van down at the Inn?"

"It is," Josie said. "Have a safe trip. You be a good girl, Velcro."

"And try to stay out of the middle of the street," I called out.

We watched them walk down to the Inn and waited until they pulled out of the parking lot. We gave them a final wave as they disappeared from sight.

"I feel like hanging out all day," I said. "Maybe do some reading. Or find something on TV we can binge on."

Josie gave me a coy smile but said nothing.

"What?" I said.

"Aren't you forgetting something?"

I frowned and gave her question some thought. Then I shook my head.

"I don't think so."

Josie gestured at Chef Claire who was heading our way. She was dressed in full workout gear.

"Crap," I whispered. "I completely forgot."

"Are you ready?" Chef Claire said, stretching her legs to warm up.

"It's Saturday," I said.

"So?" she said, sliding down into a full split.

"So, it's the weekend. And since the insane exercise program you've got me on is unbelievably hard work, shouldn't we wait until it's actually a work day?"

"Nice try," Chef Claire, effortlessly returning to a standing position. "Let's go."

"Shouldn't you be at the restaurant?" I said.

"Not until dinner," she said through a crocodile smile. "C'mon, go get changed."

"I don't want to," I said, pouting.

"Didn't you say you'd kill to have a six-pack like Imelda?" Chef Claire said, bouncing in place on her tiptoes.

"I changed my mind," I said. "I thought I'd go for the pony keg."

They both laughed, but Chef Claire was relentless.

"Move your butt," she said.

I wiggled in place.

"There. Are we done?"

"Don't make me get my bat," Chef Claire said. "Josie is going to keep an eye on Max while we're gone. And the sooner we start, the sooner it will be over."

"What's on the schedule today?" I said, unsure I wanted to hear the answer.

"A three-mile powerwalk followed by a trip to the gym. We'll be working on your core."

"Three miles? Are you out of your frigging mind?"

"You want to make it five?" she said, raising an eyebrow at me.

"Fine," I snapped. "But you know I suck at this stuff, right?"

"Really? I hadn't noticed," Chef Claire deadpanned.

"Funny."

"Go change," she commanded.

"You do know that this exercise program falls well outside my new theory about how to lead a successful life."

"Go."

"Slave driver," I muttered as I handed Max to Josie and kissed my daughter on the forehead. "It was nice knowing you, kid."

"And no dawdling or snacking," Chef Claire said.

Conceding defeat, I threw up my hands and began lumbering up the driveway toward the house. Still pouting, I headed for my bedroom.

"Maybe I'll eventually get good at it and learn to like it," I said to myself in the mirror as I dug through my dresser in search of workout clothes. I slipped into my outfit then took a step back and stared into the mirror a second time.

"I look like a gym teacher gone to seed."

I gently poked my belly then shook my head.

"Instead of working out, I suppose I could cut down on the food."

I stifled a snort and shook my head.

"Nah, who am I kidding?"

I knelt down to tie my running shoes.

Made in the USA
Middletown, DE
23 March 2019